Alvin's Swap Shop

by CLIFFORD B. HICKS

Illustrations by Lisl Weil

SCHOLASTIC BOOK SERVICES
NEW YORK • TORONTO • LONDON • AUCKLAND • SYDNEY • TOKYO

for BEN

Text copyright © 1976 by Clifford B. Hicks.
Illustrations copyright © 1977 by
Scholastic Magazines Inc. This edition is
published by Scholastic Book Services, a
division of Scholastic Magazines, Inc., by
arrangement with Holt, Rinehart and Winston.

12 11 10 9 8 7 6 5 4 3 2 1   11   7 8 9/7 0 1 2/8

Printed in the U. S. A.   06

Contents

Elmira the Ant

It was an ordinary ant crawling steadily across the sidewalk as though it had very important business in the grass on the other side. True, it *was* a bit bigger than most black ants. Perhaps that's what made Alvin notice it.

Alvin Fernald and Shoie Shoemaker were seated on the steps in front of Alvin's house. It was one of the golden days of summer; the sun peered across Mrs. Nickel's roof and burned down on the boys' backs. Alvin felt warm and good, inside and out, because it was the first day of summer vacation.

He and Shoie were discussing a prob-

1

lem — a rather pleasant problem. For a whole semester they had been looking forward to vacation, and now that it was here, they couldn't decide what to do with it. The vacation stretched like a broad, smooth highway down the whole length of summer, and they couldn't make up their minds how to spend the very first morning.

"We could go swimming in Three Oaks Pond," suggested Shoie. Even though they were both twelve, Shoie was at least three inches taller than Alvin, broader through the shoulders, and one of the best swimmers in town. In fact, he was known as the Greatest Athlete in Roosevelt School.

"Water's probably still too cold," objected Alvin.

"We could hunt mushrooms in Wideman's woods."

"They're probably all gone by now."

"Gee, Alvin. Why don't you come up with some ideas? You're the guy who's supposed to have the Magnificent Brain."

Indeed Alvin's brain was magnificent. The ideas it concocted got him into all kinds of scrapes and adventures — and got him out too. When Alvin walked down the street, some adults crossed over to the other side just to avoid any chance of getting involved in another of Alvin's wild escapades.

Shoie's words were a challenge to the Magnificent Brain. Alvin reached up and tugged slowly on the lobe of his right ear, which was a sure sign the Brain was slipping into gear.

Finally he said, "I'll tell you what. I'll just show you that the Magnificent Brain can come up with a great idea, especially when it's heated up by this warm weather. I'm going to close my eyes, and when I open them, I'll have one of the greatest ideas I've ever had. Why, it'll be such a great idea that it probably will keep us busy all summer."

Alvin was instantly sorry he'd bragged. He hadn't the slightest idea what they could do all summer. Too often he was inclined to make bold statements he couldn't back up.

"Great!" said Shoie. He rubbed his hands expectantly. "Go ahead. Close your eyes."

Alvin closed his eyes, silently praying for an idea. At that moment his sister came skipping around the corner of the house. "Hi, Shoie," she said. "Why's Alvin asleep so early in the morning?"

Alvin's eyes flew open. He exploded. "Dog-

3

gone it, Pest, can't you ever leave us alone?"

She sat down beside Shoie, pigtails glowing like golden strands of rope. "Now, Alvin. Remember what Daddy said. He said you should treat me just like a human being. I know he was joking when he said it, but he meant it." She smiled sweetly at him. "So you have to be nice to me."

Her name was Daphne, but he frequently called her the Pest because she was always tagging along after him, trying to do everything he did. He recognized that this interest in his activities was a form of flattery. Actually, he enjoyed having her tag along on most of his adventures. It made him feel like a big shot. He'd never let her know that, though.

"Get lost!" he said.

"Why did you have that goofy look on your face, with your eyes all screwed shut, Alvin?"

"The Magnificent Brain was getting an idea," explained Shoie. "It's going to be a great idea that will keep us busy all summer."

"Oh, good! Go ahead, Alvin. I want to watch."

"Yeah," said Shoie. "Go ahead. I'll bet

4

you can't really get a great idea in the next sixty seconds."

Again Alvin was challenged. "I can too! You guys just be quiet, so I can think hard."

He squeezed his eyes tightly shut again. Sometimes his Magnificent Brain appeared to be a big television set, with ideas flickering rapidly across it. But this time, he saw no lights, nothing but blackness. He squeezed his eyes so tightly they hurt. This made a few flashes of green lightning zap across the TV screen, but no ideas at all.

What could he do? Admit he'd been bluffing?

When he opened his eyes, the first thing he saw was the large black ant strolling across the sidewalk in front of his toe.

"I've got it!" he exclaimed.

"What?" shouted Shoie and the Pest.

"First we have to catch the ant," he said, pointing toward his toe.

"Catch the ant," repeated the Pest. She frequently repeated the last phrase she heard.

The kids got down on their hands and knees around the ant.

"What can you do with a little old ant

all summer?" asked the Pest. She was obviously disappointed.

"Just wait and see. First we have to catch it." To tell the truth, Alvin had no idea what they could do with the ant. He was just playing for time.

Shoie reached for the ant, and it veered toward Alvin.

"I think you're just spoofing us, Alvin," said Daphne.

Alvin reached out and covered the ant with his hand very carefully so he wouldn't hurt it. "You just wait and see," he said, thinking desperately. "First I need something to put this ant in. Daphne, run upstairs to the bathroom. Inside the medicine cabinet there's a glass tube with my new toothbrush in it. Take out the brush and bring the tube down here."

While she was gone, Alvin could feel the ant wriggling under his palm.

"What are we going to do with it, old bean?" asked Shoie. He was genuinely interested.

"Just wait and see, old man," answered Alvin.

The front door slammed and the Pest came hopping down the front steps two at a time. "Here it is."

Alvin took the glass tube in his left hand. He raised the palm of his right hand, uncovering the ant. The insect staggered across the sidewalk toward Shoie, then veered back toward Alvin. Very gently Alvin picked it up between his thumb and forefinger, and dropped it into the tube. It lay there on the bottom, legs waving feebly in the air.

"Okay. Now what?" asked Shoie.

Alvin had no idea now what. He put his thumb over the top of the tube, and gazed off into the distance. A boy came trotting around the corner of Oak Street. Alvin's eyes snapped into focus. It was Turkey Otto.

"I know what we're going to do," he said urgently in a low voice. "But I don't have time to tell you now. I want you guys to back me up in everything I say to Turkey. Got it? Now look at the ant as though it's something really special." All three kids gazed at the bottom of the glass tube.

Indeed a remarkable picture *had* flashed across the tube inside the Magnificent Brain. Alvin had the first glimmering of an idea.

He heard Turkey's footsteps slow down, then come to a stop.

"Hi," said Turkey. "Whatcha looking at?"

7

Turkey was one year younger than Alvin and Shoie. His nickname fitted him fine; whenever he was excited, he made funny little gobbling sounds in his throat. Turkey was known as the "biggest believer" in Roosevelt School. You could tell Turkey anything at all, and if you said it with a straight face he'd believe you, no matter how outlandish it was. Then he'd go gobbling off to tell someone else what he'd just heard.

"An ant," Alvin replied in a special low voice. He moved the glass tube closer to his right eyeball. Obediently, Shoie and the Pest moved in closer to the tube.

"What's so special about an ant?" asked Turkey doubtfully.

"Nothing's special about *an* ant. But something's very special about *this* ant."

"What's special?" Turkey tried to see past Shoie's head.

"Her name is Elmira."

"So you have an ant named Elmira. So what's so special about that?" Turkey leaned forward, studying the ant in the bottom of the tube.

To add a bit of suspense, Alvin let about thirty seconds go by. Then he said, "Elmira is a trained ant."

8

"Yeah, a *trained* ant," echoed the Pest, genuine awe in her voice. She looked at Elmira with renewed respect.

"Yeah, she does tricks," offered Shoie.

"What kind of tricks?" Turkey moved even closer.

Another long pause. "I've taught her quite a few tricks so far, and she's practicing others," said Alvin.

"Show me a trick." Turkey's mouth stayed open. He gobbled faintly.

"I don't know," said Alvin doubtfully. "I don't think she's ready to perform for an audience yet."

"Please," begged Turkey.

"Well, okay. I'll try." Alvin lowered his voice so that it took on an air of mystery and importance. He spaced out his words. *"Elmira is the only ant in the world trained to walk upside down!"*

Turkey gasped and gobbled at the same time, which produced a very strange sound. The Pest choked back a laugh.

Alvin held the glass tube up to the sunlight, then slowly tipped it over until it was lying on its side. Elmira fell forward and strugged to her feet. She still seemed a bit dazed by her capture. She wandered errati-

9

cally down the floor of the glass tube.

"Now watch!" Alvin whispered the words, but with great emphasis. He flipped the glass tube over, so Elmira now was walking upside down along the top. "See, Turkey? *Here's an ant that can walk upside down!"*

"Gosh!" Turkey gobbled.

Alvin glanced across the tube at him. Turkey's eyes were wide.

"She can do other tricks too."

"I've never heard of an ant that can walk upside down. What else can she do?"

By now, Elmira had finished her upside-down stroll along the top of the tube. Alvin wiggled the tube ever so slightly, so it could hardly be noticed. Elmira fell to the floor and lay there on her back, her legs waving feebly in the air.

"See!" Alvin said triumphantly. "She can roll over and play dead, just like a trained dog! Look at her! See?"

"Gosh! Gobble, gobble-gobble! Hey, Alvin, will you show me how to train an ant? I'd give 'most anything to have a real live trained ant."

There was a long pause while they all watched Elmira roll over tipsily and stand up. She stood there swaying.

"She's going into her drunk act now," announced Alvin, as though he had a microphone in his hand. As Elmira walked along the floor of the glass tube, he wiggled his hand very slightly. Elmira staggered back and forth.

"Almost anything!" repeated Turkey. "I'd give almost anything for an ant like that!"

"Anything?" asked Alvin, looking at Turkey out of the corner of his eyes.

"Just about anything. Gobble!"

"How about your collection of dead spiders?"

There was a long pause. Turkey's dead spiders were famous all over town. A tiny bead of sweat ran down Turkey's face. "Yeah, even my dead spiders. I'm kinda sick of them anyway. They don't really *do* anything, like a trained ant, and Mom says I have to get rid of them."

"It's a deal," said Alvin. Then, trying to make it sound more businesslike, he said, "It's an even swap. I give you Elmira, just as you see her in this jar, for your dead spider collection. Let's go over to your house and get the spiders."

"Let me carry Elmira," begged Turkey as they headed down the street.

"Not on your life. A swap is a swap. You can have Elmira as soon as I get the spiders. But on the way over to your house I'll tell you some more tricks Elmira can do."

"Gobble, gobble."

"Gobble!" echoed the Pest. There was a big grin on her face as she looked up at Shoie.

The Swapping Starts

The kids were on their way back from Turkey's house, Alvin proudly bearing a cigarbox full of dead spiders, when he spotted Theresa Undermine sitting on her front steps. Theresa's round little face, framed in coal-black hair, normally was smiling like a jack-o'-lantern. Now, though, her eyes were downcast. She looked so sad that Alvin imagined there was a little thundercloud hanging just above her head.

Alvin had an idea.

If there was one thing that Theresa Undermine liked more than anything else it was insects. The walls of her room were decorated with butterflies and moths, with caterpillars and beetles.

"Hi, Theresa," he said, and turned up her sidewalk.

She didn't reply.

"You look pretty sad," said the Pest.

Still no reply.

Alvin held the cigarbox right in front of Theresa's eyes. "Bet you can't guess what I have in here."

Dead silence. "Cat got your tongue?" asked the Pest.

Theresa looked up. "How'd you know?" she said dully. "That's exactly right. The cat's got my tongue."

Alvin didn't know what she meant, but this wasn't the Theresa that he'd known for eight years. He felt sorry for her. "Here. Let me show you what's inside." He flipped back the lid of the box. Then he stuck his forefinger inside and stirred up all the dead spiders.

"Oh, Alvin!" Theresa's face lighted up for a moment. "Oh, Alvin, aren't they beautiful!"

"Here," he said roughly. "You can hold the box yourself."

She seemed a little baffled. "There's only one spider collection this big in town. These

14

must be Turkey's spiders. How come you've got them?"

"They're mine now."

"Ours now," repeated the Pest. Alvin gave her a sharp look.

"We traded a trained ant to Turkey," announced Shoie proudly.

"Oh, I'd give anything for these spiders," Theresa said.

"Anything?" asked Alvin. "Such as?"

"Such as — such as — " Suddenly Theresa's eyes opened wide. "Wait here, Alvin. I'll show you what I'll give you for your spider collection. Now, don't go away."

She disappeared into the house, and came back a moment later carrying a cardboard carton. She placed it on the top step. Inside, five balls of fur were rolling around — five little black and white kittens playing together.

"Oh, they're adorable!" squealed the Pest. "Oh, I just love them." Alvin tried to pet one. It climbed up the front of his shirt, scratched his nose, and sat down on top of his head.

"Alvin," said Theresa. There was a long pause. "Alvin, I'll give you all five kittens for your dead spiders."

Alvin looked across at her. A cold, calculating look came into his eye. "Welllll. I dunno. That spider collection is mighty valuable." He pretended to think, looking back and forth from the spiders to the kittens. Finally he said, "Okay. It's a trade." He held out his hand, and Theresa shook it.

Her usual big smile once again spread across her face. She closed the lid on the spiders and tightly clasped the box with both hands. She looked slyly up at Alvin. "Maybe I should tell you the reason I was so sad. At breakfast, Mom and Dad said that Sheba's kittens are old enough to get along without her now, and insisted that I get rid of them. I really am sad, you know, to see them go. But I still have Sheba, and now I know the kittens will be in good hands." A pause. "And besides," she said brightly, "now I have the best spider collection in town."

"Alvin, let's take the kittens home and see if Mom will let us keep them." The Pest was still snuggling one of the little balls of fur.

"I know my folks won't let me have one," Shoie said.

"I don't think we're going to keep any of them," said Alvin. There was a faraway look in his eye. The Magnificent Brain had taken over again. When he snapped out of his trance, he noticed the disturbed look on Theresa's face. "But don't worry. I promise we'll find good homes for them."

Instead of heading for home, Alvin turned up Hickory Street. Shoie and the Pest followed.

"Where we going, Alvin?" asked Daphne.

"We're going into business."

"But I mean *where* are we going?"

"We're going a lot of places. First, we're going over to see old Mrs. Lodwick."

"Why?" asked Shoie. "What kind of business are we in?"

"Don't you see?" said Alvin. "We've been working at it all morning. We traded Elmira, an ordinary little black ant, for a spider collection. We swapped the spider collection for five live kittens. Now we're going to swap the kittens one by one, for something even more valuable."

"Like what?"

"I don't know yet. That all depends upon what people are *willing* to swap." He paused. "There's one important thing to remember in the swapping business. *Always swap for something more valuable than what you're offering*. We're on our way to old Mrs. Lodwick's because she loves cats. She may give us something really valuable for one of them. Then we'll try some of the kids over on Highland Avenue, and by then I may have some other ideas on what to swap them for."

It was late in the morning. Alvin was still carrying the carton, but inside there were no kittens.

Mrs. Lodwick had been entranced with one of the kittens, and offered $2.50 for it. To Daphne and Shoie's amazement, Alvin had said no, and asked what else she had to offer. He'd finally swapped one kitten for 128 old phonograph records dating back to the 1930's. The other kids thought he'd climbed out of his skull.

Over on Highland Avenue, Mike Shuck had swapped them his father's old tuxedo (which no longer fit his father) for a kitten. After a great deal of haggling, David Casper, who owned the dime store and wanted a cat to watch for mice, had swapped eight hula hoops for another.

Lisa Linkletter had offered a stuffed owl, its big wings spread menacingly, which

18

Alvin had instantly traded for. And the Widow O'Brien, lonesome since her dog had died, swapped her old white wig (she now had a new brown one) for the smallest kitten of the litter.

The kids made a strange procession as they headed home for lunch. Alvin led the way wearing the tuxedo jacket and carrying the box, which now contained old phonograph records and the tuxedo pants. The glass eyes of the dusty old owl glared out of the top of the box.

Next came Shoie, a once-white wig, now turning yellow, perched atop his head.

And bringing up the rear came Daphne, trying her best to master the art of twirling eight hula hoops at one time.

Trader Fernald, World's Greatest Swapper

By early evening, when the kids were called in for dinner, Alvin was well launched on his new career. He wasn't quite prepared for the conversation at the dinner table, though.

"Where are you kids getting all that junk that's scattered across the front yard?" asked Mom.

"Yeah, I wondered the same thing," said Dad, still dressed in his uniform. He was a sergeant in the Riverton Police Department. "When I came up the front walk I tripped over what looks like an old snare drum. What in the world is it?"

"An old snare drum," said Alvin, through a mouthful of potatoes and gravy.

"And didn't I see an old coil of garden hose, a rusty wheelbarrow, and an attic fan out there?"

"Yep, Dad. You sure did. We got the attic fan from Mr. Smidley, in return for Mr. Shuck's tuxedo pants. We were lucky they just fit Mr. Smidley. Also there's an ice chest for picnics and a couple of bicycle tires out there."

"Where did you get all that stuff, son?"

"Swapped for it. That's my new business. I'm now known as 'Trader Fernald, World's Greatest Swapper.'"

Alvin's mother sighed. This could only lead to trouble. "I hope you're not using your allowance to buy all that stuff."

"He got it all with one little black ant," piped up Daphne. "He traded the ant for some spiders, and the spiders for some hula hoops and all kinds of things."

Mom gazed through her glasses at him. Alvin couldn't quite make up his mind whether it was one of her I'm-proud-of-you looks or one of her you'd-better-shape-up-or-you'll-be-in-trouble looks. Maybe it was a little bit of each.

"Alvin, you can't just leave all that stuff on the front lawn. It looks like we're running a junkyard."

"But it'll only be there until I swap it for something else, something better."

"And where are you going to keep that something else, whatever it is?" asked Dad.

"Well, I — well — "

"I can see that this swapping is fun for you," said Dad. "And as a matter of fact, it probably is good experience. But I'm going to have to lay down the law. No more swapping until you find a place — somewhere other than the front lawn — where you can keep that stuff while you're in the process of trading it off. That's final. No more swapping without a swap shop. Understand?"

"Yes, Dad."

"Now eat your green beans," said Mom.

Alvin put two green beans into his mouth and quickly chased them with a dill pickle. He was thinking furiously. Finally he glanced across at his father. "Dad, you know how you've been wanting a car-top carrier, so you can haul lumber and plywood and other big stuff?"

"Yes. It certainly would come in handy."

"There's one behind the evergreens in the front yard. It's in fine shape too. All it needs is a coat of paint."

Dad put down his fork. "Why, Alvin. That's fine. We certainly can use that."

"What's it worth to you, Dad?"

"What do you mean?"

"Well, it's mine. It isn't yours. But you want it. So what's it worth to you?"

"Well, I — well." Dad carefully took another helping of pot roast, obviously to gain time. "I suppose it's worth two or three dollars to me." Then he added hastily, "But not a penny more."

Alvin pretended to give it some thought. Finally he said, "I'll tell you what I'll do, Dad. You know that old record player in the basement? The one that came from Grandma's house?"

"Sure. To tell the truth, I don't know why we saved it. It won't play any of the records that are made today."

"That's right. It's not worth much, but I'd kind of like to have it anyway."

"Why, son?"

"Well, I've got a stack of records that were made a good many years ago. I think that record player will play them." He scattered the rest of the green beans around his plate so it would look like there weren't many left. "I'll tell you what I'll do, Dad. I'll swap that car-top carrier for the record player."

"Say, that's a pretty good deal, Alvin. Now this Saturday I want to haul enough paneling from the lumber yard to cover the east wall of Daphne's bedroom. As soon as I've finished that, I want to go get some fence posts and —"

"You mean it's a deal, Dad? The car-top carrier for the record player?"

"Sure."

Alvin modestly looked down at his plate. There was a warm glow in the middle of his stomach, where the green beans nestled beneath the dill pickle. Trader Fernald, the World's Greatest Swapper, had done it again.

"Oh, Alvin," said Daphne with a sigh. Then she started giggling. Their folks didn't know what she was giggling about.

The Key to the Door

Early the next morning, before Daphne was even awake, Alvin rode his bike out Center Street to the edge of town. He whipped through the gate of the Riverton Oil Products Company and skidded to a stop in front of a one-story building, flanked on each side by big gasoline storage tanks.

Mr. Tubbs was standing in the doorway, a cup of coffee in his hand and a toothpick in one corner of his mouth. Mr. Tubbs always had a toothpick in his mouth. He was called Tubby by everyone in Riverton, not only because of his name, but also because he was as skinny as a fence post. His name was a joke, and Tubby seemed to enjoy it as much as anyone.

"Hi, Tubby," said Alvin.

"Greetings, Alvin," the man said, smiling. Tubby was an old friend of Alvin's dad. "Haven't seen you since your robot got loose and wandered down Highway 14. What brings you around?"

"Not much," said Alvin. He stood astride his bike, kicking the dirt with his foot. "How've you been?"

"Can't complain."

"Still belong to that square-dance club?"

"Yep. We're a pretty lively bunch for people mostly in their sixties. We rent the high school gym every two weeks. You should come over and watch sometime, Alvin."

"I'll do that. Pretty good music?"

"You put your finger on a problem, Alvin." The toothpick, powered by some mysterious force, rolled over to the other side of his mouth. "You have to pay a pretty penny to get a decent dance band anymore. And then they play all the *modern* country and western stuff, not any of those real old-time hoedown tunes we like to hear."

"How's business?"

"Not bad in the big gas stations. All the little ones are in trouble. I've had to close a couple."

"Yeah. I noticed you've boarded up that old station on Main Street, right on the edge of the downtown area."

"Can't understand why, with a location like that, the station began losing money. Guess you have to be near a big shopping center or on a highway interchange to make a go of it these days."

"Now that you've closed that Main Street station, what are you going to do with the building?"

"I dunno. I've tried to rent it, but nobody's interested."

There was a long pause. Finally Alvin blurted, "I'd like to rent that station from you, Tubby."

The man looked at him sharply. "Why?"

"I'd rather not say." Then he hastened to add, "But I won't damage anything, and I'll keep everything looking just fine, even better than it is now. Cross my heart."

A smile crossed Tubby's face. "What do you think you can afford in the way of rent, Alvin?"

"Well, it's this way. I can't exactly afford

to pay you any money. But I have this old record player, see. It belongs to me. And I also have 128 old dance records, most of them made for square dancing. Maybe we could work out some kind of a swap."

The toothpick rapidly rolled across Tubby's mouth to the far side, then all the way back again. He was definitely interested. Alvin could see it in his eyes. Alvin had the odd feeling he was out at Three Oaks Pond, and a perch was beginning to play around with his hook.

"You say you'll swap the record player and all those dance records for the use of my station?"

The fish had taken the bait. Alvin gave a little tug to set the hook. "Well, I'll let you use the record player and records for as long as you let me use the building. We wouldn't exactly trade. You'd just lend me something, and in return, I'd lend you something."

"How soon can I hear the records?"

"As soon as I can get Shoie to help me bring them here."

"And you promise you won't do any damage to my property?"

"Hope to die."

Tubby reached into his pocket. He pulled out a ring of keys, found a particular one, and pulled it off the ring. The fish was hooked and practically on the stringer.

"All right, Alvin. You've always been an honest kid. I'll give you the key now. It fits both doors of the station. But you have to promise to give it back to me if the record player doesn't work, or if I don't like the records."

Tubby flipped the key into the air. It caught the morning sunlight and came plummeting down into Alvin's palm. Alvin put it in his pocket.

"I promise," he said. "After all, a deal is a deal — to the World's Greatest Swapper." He whirled his bike around and headed out the gate.

"Turkey in the Straw"

As soon as Alvin reached home he rounded up Shoie and Daphne, and told them his plans. They were overwhelmed by his ambition.

"Wow! That Magnificent Brain is working overtime," exclaimed Shoie.

They hauled the old record player up out of the basement and carefully balanced it on Daphne's red wagon. She pulled the wagon, while Alvin and Shoie each carried a carton of records.

Tubby was eagerly waiting in the doorway. He offered each of the kids a bottle of pop from the cooler he kept in his office.

30

"Now for the big test," he said. He put the record player on his desk, and plugged it in. Picking the top record off the stack, he put it on the player and flipped the switch. After a long warm-up period (so long it made Alvin nervous), the lively strains of "Turkey in the Straw" came, loudly but scratchily, from the speaker.

Tubby's eyes lighted up. He turned the volume still higher. The music was shrill and wavery, but Tubby was entranced. He grabbed Daphne around the waist and twirled her around the room. Within three minutes he had her do-si-doing and prom-enading all around the office. His eyes had taken on a wild look, and each time a record ended he could hardly wait to put on another.

Finally Alvin said, "Tubby, we have to be going now."

"Sure, sure!" Tubby paid no attention. He was looking through the stack of records, making clucking sounds of approval over each one.

"Take good care of my record player," said Alvin.

Finally Tubby turned around. "Oh, I will, Alvin, I will!" He caressed the cabinet of the player. "Cross my heart. I'll take good care of it."

31

"Thanks for the dance," said the Pest.

"Thanks for the pop," said Shoie.

"Thanks for the Swap Shop," said Alvin softly.

By noon Shoie and Daphne had cleaned up the old gas station. First they'd pried the boards off the windows, and Daphne cleaned the glass with some rags she found in a closet. Shoie swept out and then hosed down the whole station. The building consisted of a small office, a much larger area that had been used for the servicing of cars, and two rest rooms.

Alvin left them at their clean-up work and raced off on his bike. He was intent on another swapping deal, but before he could swap, he needed *something* to swap. He headed home.

Mom was weeding the flowerbed under the front window. "Mom," Alvin said abruptly and breathlessly, "I'll keep the weeds out of that flowerbed for the next three weeks in exchange for two dozen of your chocolate-chip cookies."

She smiled up at him. "That's a pretty good swap you're proposing. I'd take you up on it, but I can't let you make yourself sick eating two dozen cookies at once."

"Oh, they're not for me. For somebody else. Is it a deal?"

"It's a deal."

Alvin went inside, found a paper sack, and took it to the cooky jar. Carefully he counted out twenty-four of the biggest cookies.

As he rode away his mother called after him, "Don't forget, Alvin! You have to get all that junk out of the front yard before your father comes home tonight!" And then, as an afterthought, "And when are you going to weed my flowerbed?"

Alvin burst through the door of the Milford Lumber Company. Mr. Milford was standing behind the counter.

"Hi, Mr. Milford, I need a board about three feet long and a foot wide, and I need a small can of red paint, and I need a small paintbrush. I don't have any money."

"Whoa, Alvin. Whoa. At least slow down a little. Now, how do you expect to buy those things without any money? We're not in business to give stuff away, you know.

"I know. But I'm ready to swap."

"What do you have to swap?"

"This." Alvin opened the bag and held it close under Mr. Milford's nose, which instantly started twitching. Mr. Milford's wife had died five years ago, and since then he'd eaten every meal at McAllister's Drug Store, which wasn't known for its outstanding food.

"They're homemade," said Alvin.

"Hmmmmmm. Homemade cookies. What kind?"

"Chocolate chip."

"How many?"

"Two dozen."

Mr. Milford obviously was getting hungry. "And what was it you wanted?"

"A board, a small can of red paint, and a paintbrush."

"You drive a hard bargain, Alvin." He sniffed the cookies again. "Free sample?"

A long pause. "Yes. But just one."

Mr. Milford took a small bite out of one of the cookies. He rolled his eyes toward the ceiling. Carefully he put the cooky back in the bag, then turned and walked into the backroom without saying a word. When he returned, he was carrying a can of paint, a brush, and a piece of plywood.

"Here you are, Alvin. Just what you asked for."

Alvin picked up his new property and

turned to leave. Then he turned around, looked at the bag of cookies, and asked, "Free sample?"

"Not on your life." Mr. Milford quickly closed the bag.

The Swap Shop

A week later the Swap Shop was the talk of Riverton.

The old service station had been transformed. The walls were washed, the windows gleamed like jewels, and the concrete floor had been scrubbed a dozen times to clean off the ancient oil stains. They had shoved the drum of old engine oil into one corner and covered it with boards, then used the boards as a table to display their wares. In another corner they'd found a creeper, which Tubby had left behind, and was particularly helpful.

"What's a creeper?" Daphne had asked

when they'd first come across it and Alvin called it by name. It was built like a sled except it had tiny wheels on the bottom instead of runners.

"It's for a mechanic to work beneath a car," explained Alvin. "He lies on his back on the creeper, and can scoot anywhere he wants to go."

The kids used the creeper to haul heavy items into place in the Swap Shop.

Mom's chocolate-chip cookies had paid off in the form of a magnificent sign, which now gleamed in the morning sunlight. Alvin, as always, had slopped on too much paint; the letters appeared to be oozing blood. But Alvin thought the sign had a real touch of class:

"ALVIN'S OLD-TIME SWAP SHOP — If we don't have what you want, we'll get it for you!"

It was a fine motto, and it attracted business like a bruised apple attracts bees.

Their first customer was old Mr. Jimsen. He had, perhaps, the greatest curiosity in town — he was always nosing around to see what anyone and everyone was doing — and he had plenty of time for nosing, because he had retired from the waterworks.

He carried a cane, not because he was crippled, but as a prod or poker that he could use to satisfy his curiosity.

The kids had been in high spirits on this, their first day of business, and Alvin had just unlocked the Swap Shop door when Mr. Jimsen approached, his nose twitching as though he was a hunting dog on the trail of something big.

"Hello, there, Alvin. Daphne. You, too, Wilfred." Mr. Jimsen knew everyone in town. He stood just outside the door. "What are you kids up to? Did Tubby give you permission to play around this old station?"

"Hi, Mr. Jimsen," responded Alvin. He glanced at the other kids. "Sure. Tubby knows we're here. In fact, we're renting this building from him. In a way."

Mr. Jimsen poked his head through the doorway, then stepped inside the biggest of the two rooms. "What are you kids doing in here?"

"Didn't you see our sign?" asked Alvin. He was proud of it, and couldn't believe Mr. Jimsen hadn't seen it.

"Yep. Something about a swap store."

"Swap Shop," corrected Daphne.

"What's a Swap Shop?"

Mr. Jimsen's eyes swept the contents of the room. There were two old lawnmowers in one corner, also a short length of hose, some rakes, two hoes, one shovel, and a popcorn popper. Along one wall the kids had stacked empty lettuce crates to build a series of shelves. The shelves held dishes, silverware, kitchen utensils, a box of old yo-yos, toys, and games.

Indeed the kids had been very busy for an entire week, swapping one thing for two in a successful effort to stock the Swap Shop.

"What do you kids intend to do with all this junk?" Mr. Jimsen poked his cane into a doll's stomach. Surprisingly, the doll said, "Maaaaammmaaaaa!"

"I didn't know that doll could talk!" exclaimed Daphne.

"Neither did I!" said Shoie.

Alvin watched as Mr. Jimsen poked his cane into a box of old nuts and bolts. "You see, we're in the swapping business," he explained. "You're really our very first official customer, but we've been swapping for a week to build up our stock."

Mr. Jimsen was squatting down beside a lettuce crate. "Where did you get this bowl of tropical fish?" he asked. There was a sudden edge of interest in his voice. Alvin knew that Mr. Jimsen's aquarium was the pride of his life.

"We traded Worm Wormley a pair of roller skates for eight of those fish. Worm wanted the roller skates to build a box scooter."

"How much do you want for the fish?"

"We're not in business to make money, Mr. Jimsen. At least not yet. This is a Swap Shop. What can you offer us for the fish?"

Mr. Jimsen obviously was excited. "Well. Well, I have three gallons of homemade dill pickles."

"What else?" asked Alvin promptly.

"An old trombone. To be honest, though, I should tell you that it's beat up. Full of dents. Big dents."

"It's a deal," said Alvin.

"What's a deal?"

"We'll swap you the tropical fish for the dill pickles and the trombone."

Mr. Jimsen stood up. He looked at Alvin. "I don't want to gyp you. You should know that *one* of these tropical fish is quite rare. And therefore very valuable." He held the bowl up to the sunlight streaming through the open door. "A real beauty!"

"It's still a deal." Alvin stuck out his hand, and Mr. Jimsen shook it briefly.

Alvin said, "Shoie, you and Pest go get the pickles and the trombone while I watch the store."

That's the way it had gone, for a week now. The motto, *"If we don't have what you want, we'll get it for you,"* had really drawn in the business.

Dr. Gibson had noticed the sign, and came in seeking a headlight for a 1927 car he was restoring. Alvin had finally located one in old Mrs. Hunter's garage, and traded her a huge box of used Christmas cards for it. In turn, he had swapped Dr. Gibson out of a first-aid kit, twenty-one rolls of adhesive tape, and a certificate good for one free office call. Alvin had promptly swapped the office-call certificate to Mrs. Throttlemorton, who enjoyed bad health, for a ball of used aluminum foil eighteen inches in diameter.

Mildred Reimer came in looking for a quilting frame. Eventually she walked out with the quilting frame (the kids had been lucky to find one in Mrs. Milton's basement) and in its place left a working chicken incubator, because she no longer raised chickens.

41

Janet Whittaker, who was a football freak, came in seeking an autographed picture of Joe Namath, "because it will be the very superist utmost of my whole collection." This swap was still in the works. For twenty-four hours Alvin had puzzled over where to obtain an autographed picture of Joe Namath. Then, in an instant of inspiration, had written Joe Namath a request for an autographed picture and had enclosed a picture of himself, carefully autographed "Alvin Fernald." He felt it was an even swap.

Yep. Things were piling up in the Swap Shop. They had just acquired two old merry-go-round horses from Mr. Eaton, who had once worked for a carnival; a small rowboat with only one hole in it from Bob Gibbons, who had a cabin on Three Oaks Pond; and a ball of red worms from Fisheye Johnson's little brother. They had traded something for each of these items, and in each case (at least in Alvin's estimation) they had come out ahead.

They received a boxful of out-of-fashion sunglasses from Old Doc Seymour, the optometrist, in exchange for an air horn for his boat. They picked up a dozen sets of earmuffs from Wart van Wert, who managed the men's clothing store on Main Street. By shrewd trading they got half a dozen used spotlights from Mr. Gizburne, who built billboards throughout the area, in exchange for a drum of roofing compound.

Mrs. Nardulli was eager to trade her big window fan (she had just air-conditioned her house) for ten rolls of wallpaper that didn't match. Myron Butz had contributed three cartons of old books for six sets of used false teeth (one set seemed to fit him slightly). Alvin was particularly proud of trading off two live gerbils to Duffy Skymer, who ran the roller skating rink, for a huge amplifier and two giant speakers, which Duffy had replaced with more modern equipment.

But perhaps the greatest swap of all involved Bernard Bezy, who had just retired and closed up the "Bezy Spectacular Joke and Novelty Store." Mr. Bezy, who had an eye for the women, traded Alvin five pounds of "Cut-Rate Itching Powder" for a statue of a nude woman without a head. Shoie had gone into a physical fit after rubbing just a bit of the powder on his stomach. "That stuff really works," he reported, after returning from home, where he'd taken a quick shower.

The kids themselves had had a lot of fun with one item. It was an exercising treadmill. Mr. Barclay had stopped in, spotted an old accordion, and offered to deliver the treadmill on his pickup truck in exchange. He'd dropped it off the same afternoon. It was so heavy that it had been a real struggle to get it inside, even on the creeper.

"What does it do?" asked the Pest, gazing at it. Basically, it was a slanting platform about six feet long, covered by an endless rubber belt. Along each side of the platform there were railings.

Alvin plugged in the electrical cord and gave Shoie the control box, which had numbers from one to ten. Alvin climbed onto the slanting platform, and seized the side rails. "Turn it to number one."

The endless belt started moving beneath his feet. Alvin had to walk along at a brisk pace just to stay in place. By the time Shoie had turned up the control to number seven, Alvin was running as hard as he could, hanging desperately onto the rails.

When the treadmill was turned off, he climbed down, out of breath, the sweat running down his face. "We'll use that every morning to keep ourselves in shape," he managed to gasp.

Alvin wasn't so sure about one swap they'd made. Bill Perry, who owned the shoe store on Main Street, had come in just to look around, and spotted 800 yards of used audio tape which had come off the spools and was lying in a snarl inside a cardboard box. He thought he could salvage it, and therefore had started dickering. As a result, Bill Perry got the tape, and the Swap Shop got thirty-four left shoes.

"Funny," Mr. Perry had mused to Alvin. "When the factory goofs, for some reason they always put two *left* shoes in a box. It's never two *right* shoes. I suppose I should be glad they don't goof very often. It's taken me twenty-six years to collect those thirty-four left shoes. In a way, I'm sorry to see them go. They make a nice little collection — maybe the biggest left-shoe collection in the world — and they're the only thing I ever collected in my life. Anyway, I really can use the audio tape if I can get it unsnarled, and I don't see how I can use those thirty-four left shoes."

Alvin didn't see how he could use them either. Maybe for the first time in the short life of the Swap Shop he'd been outswapped.

The Adventure Begins

The real Swap Shop adventure began one Tuesday morning with no warning whatever.

It was an ideal summer day, already warm, but with a pleasant breeze that showed promise of keeping it comfortable even through the afternoon.

Alvin and Daphne hurried through breakfast, anxious to open the Swap Shop for another day's business. When they arrived at the old service station, Shoie was already sitting on the front step scratching his name in the concrete with a sharp stone.

Alvin dug the key out of his pocket and,

with an unnecessary flourish, turned the lock. He swung open the door and propped it wide with an empty bucket.

The kids walked inside, totally unsuspecting, and began discussing what they should use for their "outdoor display." Each day they put a few choice items just outside the door as "Special Swap Bargains."

"Let's set up one of the merry-go-round horses," suggested the Pest. "I'll pose on it, and maybe somebody from the *Daily Bugle* will come around and take my picture. It'll be good publicity."

"Let's put out the Styrofoam ice chest," suggested Shoie. "It's shaped like a pirate's chest."

Alvin thought for a moment, then said, "The merry-go-round horse is a good idea, but we may have to —"

"AAAARRRRKKKEEEEEE!" Daphne shrieked at the top of her lungs.

Alvin grabbed her by the shoulders. Obviously she was terrified. "What's the matter, Sis?" he asked urgently. He never called her Sis unless he was serious.

Daphne pointed toward a corner of the room. She opened her mouth and tried to speak. She couldn't produce a sound.

In the corner was a stack of old flour sacks that the kids had obtained from Mr. Cortney, the baker, in exchange for a pair of earrings, which he intended to give his wife for her birthday.

"What's the matter?" Alvin asked again, squeezing her shoulders.

"There's something alive," she whispered. "Under those flour sacks." Her eyes were wide with fright.

"How do you know?" asked Shoie. He, too, was whispering.

"I saw the sacks move."

Alvin knew, deep inside, that he was no braver than the other kids; in fact, he was every bit as scared. But he also knew that they looked to him for leadership.

Knees trembling, he walked slowly over to the corner. He stooped down and stared for a long moment at the pile of flour sacks. Slowly he reached out a hand, grabbed a fistful of the sacks, and jerked them away.

There was an instant of turmoil.

Alvin shouted, "Run! Run!" but all three kids were paralyzed.

The remainder of the sacks were heaving and twisting this way and that, as though violently alive.

Then suddenly, as though from the grave, an arm reached out from beneath the sacks. It was a long, brown arm, and the fingers of the hand were spread, as though they were searching for something to hang on to. Even in his terror, Alvin noticed that the hand was covered with dirt, as if it hadn't been washed in a week. Finally the clawlike fingers grabbed the remaining flour sacks and flung them aside.

Daphne ran screaming through the front door.

Shoie shrank back into a far corner of the room.

Alvin stood motionless as a statue.

Up, up, out of the flour sacks crawled a human being. At least that's what it appeared to be. As the figure staggered to his feet and stood there blinking in the sunlight, Alvin could see that it was indeed a human being — in fact, it was a boy only slightly larger than himself. The boy had a tangled mass of curly hair, white as bones, as though it had been bleached for years in the sun. It contrasted with the deep tone of the boy's face.

He stood there rubbing his eyes. He was wearing a pair of jeans cut off high above his knees, and raveled out at the bottom. These, too, were so bleached there was scarcely a trace of color left in them. This was the only article of clothing he wore except for a pair of sneakers.

Alvin noticed that the lad was tall and slim — so thin that his ribs were beginning to show.

The stranger suddenly seemed to become aware of his situation.

"I say there," he said, looking straight at Alvin, "you really give a man a start." He seemed to be speaking a strange dialect. It was almost as though he were from England, yet his voice was very soft, and he said something that sounded like "mon" instead of "man."

"It's you who gave us a surprise," said Alvin, his eyes narrowing. "Incidentally, this is our property. At least in a way. What are you doing in here?" As he waited for an answer, he noticed that the boy's face was dirty, his hair matted.

"I was searching for some place to sleep. The window was open a wee bit, so I climbed in. Just for a few hours. I didn't think anyone would mind."

Daphne's head poked through the doorway. She took one look at the boy — at his curly blond hair and his fine features — and sighed the deepest sigh of her life. Daphne had just fallen in love.

"Maybe we *do* mind," said Alvin. "This is our Shop and you are" — he searched for the word — "trespassing. What's your name?"

"Pim. Pim Bethel."

"That's a funny name," commented Shoie. "Pim."

"I think it's a beautiful name," said Daphne. She flashed her most radiant smile.

There was a long silence. Finally Pim said, "Well, I'd best be going. Thank you for letting me stay here. I'm very sorry I startled you." He took a step toward the door.

"Wait!" said Daphne, a little too loud, as though she were desperate. "You haven't had any breakfast."

"No," said Pim. "Nor anything yesterday either. But I shan't trouble you any further."

"Well," said Alvin, trying to maintain control. "Well, this is our Swap Shop. I suppose we could find you something to eat if you have anything to swap for the food."

"I have no money."

"I didn't mean money. I mean anything to trade."

In reply, the boy turned his pockets inside out. His left hand was empty; his right hand held a small seashell.

"Oh!" squealed Daphne. "What a beautiful shell! Let me see it."

Pim held it up to the light, but did not put it in her hand. It was an oddly twisted shell, about two inches long, colored in various tints of bright orange and muted brown. A slit curled up one side.

"You *are* hungry," Alvin said. It was a statement, not a question.

"Yes. Very hungry."

"Well, Pim, we're in the swapping business." It was the first time he had used the boy's name. "Tell you what we'll do. We'll swap you a bologna sandwich, a glass of milk, and some homemade applesauce" — Alvin watched Pim's tongue come out and and lick his lips — "for that pretty little seashell."

It was almost as though he had insulted the boy. The tongue shot back into Pim's mouth, and he shook his head violently. "No!" he said. "I'll never give away the shell. For anything. Anything!"

Daphne saved the day. "Oh, come on, you guys. Let's forget about swapping. Pim's hungry. I'm going home to get him something to eat. That's all there is to it. Now, you guys sit down and get acquainted. I'll be right back."

"Wait!" said Pim urgently. "I appreciate what you are doing. And someday perhaps I can pay you back. But" — his voice took on a desperate note — "but I beg you, don't let anyone know I am here. Anyone!"

There was a long silence. Then Alvin spoke up, taking charge again. "I reckon we can do that much," he said, a smile spreading across his face, "for an honored guest. Run along, Pest. Mom's probably in the basement this morning doing the laundry. Just bring whatever you can find in the refrigerator. If Mom catches you and says anything, tell her Shoie and I are hungry. Anyway, don't say anything about Pim. At least not just yet."

"Not a word," promised Daphne, her eyes shining at the stranger. She darted out the door, intent on saving her newest love from starvation.

Within thirty minutes, Pim's spirits had been raised many notches. He'd finished off a bologna sandwich and a peanut butter sandwich, two pieces of cold fried chicken, a bowl of homemade potato salad, and half a dozen cookies. Daphne had been determined to impress him, and in turn she was impressed not only by his tremendous appetite, but by his precise manners. First he had bowed slightly as he thanked her. She'd thoughtfully provided a knife and fork, and she noticed that, as he deftly cut the chicken into small pieces, he held the fork in his left hand, and shoved the food onto it with the knife, which he held in his right hand. Then the left hand raised the fork to his mouth — *upside down.* She was entranced. It reminded her of the way she'd seen the actors eat in a movie made in England.

"Oh, Pim," she sighed, making her voice as husky as possible, "are you from England? That's so romantic."

"No, not England," he said. He abruptly changed the subject. "I really do appreciate the food. It's the first decent meal I've had in days. Someday I hope to repay you."

"Nertz!" exclaimed Alvin. "We may be swappers, but not where food is concerned."

Pim looked at each of the three kids in turn. "I owe you for a fine meal and a night's lodging already," he said. "But I have one final favor to ask. Would you mind a great deal if I stayed inside this building until darkness comes tonight?"

"Why?" asked Alvin curiously.

There was no reply for a moment. Then, "It's just as well for you that you don't know the reason."

"Are you in trouble with the law? My dad's a policeman here in Riverton."

"No. I swear. I have broken no laws. But please — if I am a burden to you I will leave right now."

"Not on your life," said Daphne, taking charge. "You're going to stay right here all day, Pim. That little room over in the corner is the bathroom. There's a sink in there, and I'll get you a towel and some soap from home. You wash up and you'll feel lots better."

"That's right, Pim," agreed Alvin. "I'll not ask any more questions. I figure you're hiding from someone. That's your own business. But in order to avoid suspicion that you're here, we'll have to keep the Swap Shop open as usual. Understand?"

"I'll be on the lookout," broke in Shoie. "Whenever a customer comes toward the door, I'll whistle like this." He did his imitation of a whippoorwill. "When you hear that, you lock yourself in the bathroom. Okay?"

Pim looked around at the three faces. "How could I have been so lucky?" he asked. Then, as though it was a ritual, he pulled the beautiful little seashell from his pocket and rubbed his thumb across its shining surface.

Scarface!

"Pim really spaces me out." Daphne sighed. "He has such dreamy eyes. I could look at him forever."

"Don't think about him," Alvin ordered. "Think about what you're doing. It looks like a blizzard behind you."

It was late in the afternoon, and the kids were heading back to the Swap Shop. They had been out swapping for what Alvin called an "incredible deal."

They'd run, just as fast as they could, out to Oostermeyer's farm on the edge of town. The reason they'd run was because they were carrying snowballs on a warm

June day. And the reason they were carrying snowballs was Jennie Oostermeyer.

Jennie had wandered into the Swap Shop that morning. (Pim had escaped into the washroom just in time.) She'd looked over the Swap Shop's valuables, and announced that she had four bushels of chicken feathers to swap, but she didn't see anything she wanted in the Swap Shop.

The chicken feathers intrigued Alvin, and he asked her what she wanted.

"A dozen snowballs," she replied, a challenge in her voice.

The Magnificent Brain came up with an answer. "Go out to the farm, Jennie," said Alvin. "Put the feathers in some cardboard boxes so we can carry them back here. We'll deliver the snowballs within an hour."

They'd locked Pim inside the Swap Shop. (Daphne was the last one out, and had whispered, "See you later, Pim.") Alvin led the way, carrying an eighteen-inch ball of aluminum foil. They went straight to Willy Davis's house. Evil Eye, Willy's little brother, was throwing a rubber ball against the garage door. His strange little eyes lighted up when he saw the aluminum ball.

"Hi," he said, catching the rubber ball

once more, then holding it this time. "Gee, Alvin, that's a mighty big ball of aluminum foil. Wish it were mine."

"What would you do with it?" asked Daphne.

"Probably sell it to Mr. Tiffleplitz." Ben Tiffleplitz owned the Riverton Junk Palace. He was an ever-present source of money to the kids in Riverton, because he would buy waste paper, aluminum foil, scrap metal, and other junk they collected.

"What'll you swap for it?" asked Alvin.

Evil Eye thought for a minute. "Well, I dunno, Alvin. How about this rubber ball?" he asked doubtfully.

"No deal. But you *do* have something I could use. I'll trade you this valuable supply of aluminum foil for a dozen snowballs."

Evil Eye was famous in Riverton for his annual mid-summer Snowball Fight. His father owned the Kwik-Kool Frozen Food Lockers. Each winter he permitted Evil Eye to pack more than a hundred snowballs into one of the big freezers. On the Fourth of July, which for some reason always seemed to be the hottest day of the year, Evil Eye would invite his closest friends over for the traditional Snowball Fight, and a good

59

many other kids would come to watch. It now was a famous event in town, and last year the *Daily Bugle* had carried a whole page of photos of the fight.

"Nope. Can't do that, Alvin. Need them for the Snowball Fight."

"Aw, c'mon, Evil. You've got more than two hundred snowballs in that freezer. I know. I helped you make them. Remember? You won't miss a dozen of them."

The kids argued for ten minutes before Evil Eye finally gave in. He hopped on his bike and disappeared in the direction of Kwik-Kool. Ten minutes later he was back balancing a box on his handlebars. Nested neatly inside were a dozen big, white snowballs.

"Oooohh! Let me touch them!" exclaimed Daphne.

"Not on your life," said Alvin. "That'll just make them melt. C'mon. We've got to get them out to Oostermeyer's fast!"

They'd run all the way, and arrived just in time, because little rivers of water were beginning to trickle down the sides of the snowballs. Jennie squealed with delight, and swiftly transferred them to the Oostermeyer home freezer.

Now the kids were on their way back to the shop, each carrying a big carton.

"Doggone it, Pest!" exclaimed Alvin again. "You're tipping that box again. Look behind you."

Daphne looked back over her shoulder. There was a miniature, white blizzard of chicken feathers in the air behind her. "Why couldn't Jennie have given us boxes with lids?" she complained. "Anyway, what're we going to do with all these feathers, Alvin?"

"I dunno yet," admitted Alvin. "But somehow I have a hunch they're going to be important to the Swap Shop."

They crossed Myrtle and headed up Third Street. Alvin heard the sound of a tire scraping the curb.

"Hey, kids!"

Alvin looked up. A man was hollering at them through the open window of the car.

"Yeah, you kids, there. With the boxes. C'mere a minute."

Alvin lowered the box of feathers to the sidewalk and approached the car. He was careful not to get too close, though. *Never get in a car with a stranger.* He had heard it as far back as he could remember.

"Can I help you?" he asked politely, peering into the car. Daphne and Shoie were just behind him.

"I hope so. I'm lookin' for a new kid in town. Maybe you've seen him."

Alvin looked the man over carefully, and didn't particularly like what he saw. He was perhaps twenty-five to thirty years old, with very broad shoulders. His eyes were set wide apart, so dark they appeared to be black, and they didn't seem to have any expression. But, the thing that was most noticeable of all was the deep, white scar that curved down across the man's tanned skin. Starting from his right eyebrow, it zigzagged across his cheek and extended down to the corner of his jaw. It looked like an ugly chalk line.

"What does the kid look like?" asked Alvin.

"Well, he's about your age — maybe a year or two older. Probably wearing some cut-off jeans. He has dark skin and blond hair — you can't miss that combination."

"Why, that sounds just like — " Daphne instantly shut her mouth when Alvin tromped down on the top of her foot.

"What did you say?" asked the man glancing sharply at Daphne.

"How come you're trying to find this kid?" interrupted Alvin.

"Well, it's like this. I'm his uncle, and we were just traveling through town here when he stopped off to see a friend of his, and now, well — well, I can't seem to find him."

Alvin thought the story sounded fishy. Scarface must have thought so too, because he hurriedly added, "I just want to find him so I can let him know I'm staying out at the Sleep Snug Motel, and that he can meet me there."

"If we see him, we'll tell him that," said Alvin.

"Yeah, you do that. Even better, you tell him that I have some news about his mother. Yeah. Tell him his mother is just fine — and I hope her health doesn't take a turn for the worse. Yeah, that ought to bring him running." He said the last sentence in a whisper, as though to himself. His cold, expressionless eyes shifted to Daphne, and she shrank back under that gaze. The man reached in his pocket. He waved a ten-dollar bill through the window. "I figure that anybody who does me a favor, like finding that kid, deserves a favor in return. If you kids take me to him, or bring him out to the motel, this ten-spot is yours."

Alvin turned away from the car so abruptly that he walked right into the Pest and knocked her down. Shoie pulled her quickly to her feet, and the kids picked up their boxes from the sidewalk.

"Remember, ten bucks for the kid!" called the man. Then the car gunned off and screeched around the corner.

"I don't like him," said the Pest in a soft voice. "I don't like him at all."

"Yeah." Shoie walked in silence for a moment. "Can you imagine him offering ten dollars for finding Pim? It's almost like trying to *buy* somebody. I wonder if he really is Pim's uncle."

"I hope not." Alvin repeated it with emphasis. "I certainly hope not. Pest, you started to tell him that we've seen Pim."

"But I didn't," she wailed in a small voice. "I wouldn't want to get Pim in trouble for anything in the world."

They didn't see the car again. And they weren't around, ten minutes later, when it came rolling slowly up the street.

The kids had left an easy trail to follow. Even from inside the car, Scarface could see the white ribbon of feathers stretching two blocks up Third Street, then turning onto Main.

And even from a distance the man could see the speckled white trail ending on the front step of the Swap Shop.

Pim Tells His Story

The news that Scarface was in town and looking for him terrified Pim, though he tried not to show it. Now and then he peered out one corner of a window, as though he were afraid that the man would be out there. At other times he strode back and forth inside the Swap Shop, stepping over all the junk the kids had accumulated, but always staying well to the center of the room, so he couldn't be seen from outside. Alvin noticed that the beautiful little shell was constantly in Pim's hand now, his thumb rubbing back and forth across the shiny surface as though the feel of it reassured him.

Pim stopped pacing and looked sharply across at Alvin. "You're sure he said my mother is just fine?"

"Yes. And then he said he hoped her health doesn't take a turn for the worse. That's exactly what he said. And that's the fifth time you've asked me that question, Pim. Why is he searching for you? And why don't you just go on out to the Sleep Snug Motel and ask him about your mother? Where *is* she, anyway? Why don't you tell us what's going on? Maybe we can help."

"Maybe we can help!" echoed Daphne.

"Yeah," put in Shoie. "Old Scarface out there isn't so big. I'm not afraid of him. Just lead me to him!" Shoie flexed his arms like a prizefighter.

"You *would* be afraid of him if you'd seen what I've seen," said Pim softly. He drew a deep breath and looked around at the other kids' faces. "This man is dangerous. And I don't want to involve you, my new friends." He peered out the corner of the window once more. "I'll be going now."

"You'll *not* be going now," ordered Alvin. "You're staying right here." The corners of his mouth turned up in a faint smile. "We'll keep you captive, Pim, until we find out how we can help you."

"Oh, that'll be fun." It was Daphne, of course.

"And if, as you say, this man Scarface really is dangerous, then we'll tell Dad. The whole Riverton Police Force will go after him."

"No! No!" exclaimed Pim abruptly. "That would be exactly the wrong thing to do. Then I might never see my mother again." He thought for a moment, his handsome face wrinkled with worry. "Perhaps you have a right to know." He sat down on the floor, his back to the wall.

"Tell us the whole story," said Alvin quietly. "Then we'll decide — together — what's best to do."

The Swap Shop was totally silent for a full minute.

"I suppose the story begins on an island you've probably never even heard of. It begins on Eleuthera . . ."

The Magic Shell

"Eleuthera is my home," said Pim in his softly accented voice. "It's one of the out-islands of the Bahamas, in the Atlantic Ocean, southeast of your state of Florida. The out-islands have very few people on them. They're the most beautiful islands of the Bahamas. Eleuthera must be the most beautiful out-island of all.

"We Bahamians on Eleuthera are poor, but the island is good to us. My friends and I fish, and dive, and hunt wild pineapples, and play games, and go to school when the sun is not too high." He sighed. "I wish I were there right now."

"Were you born on Eleuthera?" asked Shoie.

"Yes. My father came from the United States. He came to Eleuthera to fish, but he often told me that he fell in love with the island and my mother at the same time. She was a native Bahamian. After they were married, my father never returned to the United States.

"My father got a job as the dockmaster in Hatchet Bay. That is a village with a good harbor, where yachts and sportfishing boats from all over the world tie up for fuel, supplies, and for protection in foul weather. As dockmaster, my father supervised everything around the dock.

"I worked on the dock too. I hauled food to the boats from the store in Hatchet Bay, I swabbed down decks for pay, I filled petrol tanks, and even dived for money that the tourists tossed into the water.

"It was fun to work around my father. He was big and strong and made everyone laugh."

Pim was silent for a moment, his eyes downcast. Alvin cleared his throat self-consciously. "Pim, you talk about your father as though he's dead. Is he?"

Pim resumed talking, as though he hadn't even heard the question. "Even after he became dockmaster, he loved to fish whenever he had time. When I was eight years old he went out fishing, and never returned. A sudden storm washed his boat back to a beach far on the north side."

Shyly, Daphne reached out and touched Pim on the knee. "I'm so sorry, Pim."

Pim gazed into a far corner of the room, as though he saw something the others couldn't see. "He left me only one thing. Early one morning, a few years ago, he took me with him to dive for conch. My mother makes the best conch fritters in the world. Someday I hope you'll taste them.

"We had great fun that morning. He knew where to find the biggest conch and could bring them up from twenty or thirty feet deep. Later, as we walked along the beach, he stooped and picked up a shell. He held it up to the sunlight, and stared at it. Then he put it in my hand and closed my fingers around it.

" 'Save this shell,' he told me. 'It took nature millions of years to develop it, Pim. Maybe nature put some kind of magic inside. Let's call it your magic shell. Keep it, and perhaps you'll have good luck all your life.'

"That's why I couldn't trade the shell to you — what you call swapping? — for the food. I'll never part with the shell. It's the only thing I have left of my father . . ."

There was a long silence in the Swap Shop. No one moved. Finally Pim resumed his story. "After my father was lost, my mother sold our nice house to an American fisherman. We moved to a shack on the edge of Hatchet Bay, out by the abandoned pineapple plantation. My mother took a job in Mr. Smythe's grocery store, and I still worked around the dock — except when I was reading.

"We don't have a very good library in Hatchet Bay — just three shelves of books inside the constable's office. But reading came easy to me, and I read every word I could find about my island. There was one book I read so many times I almost memorized it. It was a history book, and told how the pirates, three hundred years ago, lay in wait, in their big ships, just off the southern tip of Eleuthera. They were waiting for Spanish galleons loaded with gold. And they sank many a galleon within a mile of where I swam.

"I enjoyed snorkeling, and once, late in the afternoon, I spotted the broken ribs of a big ship in sixty feet of clear water just below me. The next day — and many days after that — I tried finding the wreck again, but failed.

"At least I failed until last month — and I wish I'd failed then, too . . ."

A feeling of tension had crept into the Swap Shop. Alvin stood up and stretched. Without even being aware of what he was doing, he walked over to a shelf and picked up a cowboy hat he'd obtained in a swap with Texas Tremont, who ran the local pool parlor. When he put on the big hat, it fell down below his ears. Nobody laughed.

Alvin took off the hat, and placed it carefully on a shelf. "When did you first meet Scarface?" he asked quietly, returning to his place on the floor beside Pim.

Pim's thoughts were far away. "There was no way I could know that boat carried nothing but trouble when she swung wide around a freighter and made for our dock. She was a thirty-foot cruiser with a flying bridge for deep-sea fishing. A man held the bow line, but when he tried to make her fast at our dock, I could see he didn't know much about boats. I tried to give him a hand, but he only snarled at me. He had a scar that ran zigzag down the side of his face. You've seen him here in Riverton.

"When he had the boat tied up, another man came ashore. He had white hair, and was older than the man you call Scarface. He retied the lines. The boat was his. He said his name was Pogue, and he treated me just as though I were an adult.

"Mr. Pogue asked if I'd haul some tinned goods from the grocery store to the boat, and stow them in the galley. When I came back with a box full of tins, the two men were sitting on deck. Mr. Pogue nodded his head toward the galley.

"I climbed down the ladder and into the galley. It was as tidy as any I've seen, with a special place for everything. I could see through into the cabin. There was a whole shelf of books. When I'd finished stowing the tins, I stepped over to the cabin door to see what kind of books they were. There were books on everything from sailing to stamp collecting, from sharks to mountain climbing.

"I jumped when a harsh voice, from right over my shoulder, asked me what I was trying to steal. I whirled around. Somehow

74

Scarface had managed to creep silently down the ladder.

"I told him I wasn't stealing anything, that I was just looking at the names on the books. I climbed back up the ladder.

"Mr. Pogue overheard me, and asked me if I liked to read. I told him I'd read all the books in the constable's office at least twice. He asked if I'd ever read anything about the waters around Eleuthera. I mentioned the book about the pirates, and the galleons sunk off South End. I even told him about the broken ribs of the big ship I'd seen.

"Scarface and Mr. Pogue got very excited. The old man asked me if I'd be their guide, starting the next day. He offered me ten dollars a day, and a fair share of anything we found."

Shoie gave a low whistle. "That's pretty good pay, Pim. I wish I could make ten dollars in one day, just by cruising around in a neat boat."

"It's even better pay in the Bahamas. Before I had time to agree to it, Scarface complained that he wasn't splitting treasure with any kid. Then I knew they were treasure hunters. Lots of divers hunt for old wrecks around the Bahamas. Sometimes they find them too.

"Mr. Pogue said it was his boat, that he was in charge, and that if I helped them find treasure I was entitled to part of it. The odds against our finding a Spanish galleon were pretty high, he said, but he promised me a bonus, in addition to my pay, even if we found nothing. He said that as soon as he got back to Miami he'd send me a box of books.

"I told him I'd rather have the books than the money. He said I'd get both."

Pim was silent for a moment.

The question popped out of Daphne's mouth before she could even think about it. "Did you find any treasure?" she asked, an undercurrent of excitement in her voice.

"I'm coming to that," said Pim. "The next morning we ran down to South Tip. The water was calm except for long swells. Mr. Pogue was at the wheel. I laid flat on the bow, guiding him between the coral heads to the area where I'd seen the broken ribs.

"It was my bad luck that we *ever* found those broken ribs, but we did it right away. There she lay, between the two big coral heads, in sixty feet of water. I shouted, and

Mr. Pogue hove to. As soon as I pointed, he dropped anchor.

"All three of us were excited. The two men went below and came back carrying the fanciest scuba gear I'd ever seen. I could tell that Scarface was a good scuba diver as soon as he jumped into the water. One quick flip of his fins, and he was gone.

They were down about thirty minutes, and when they climbed the stern ladder, Scarface carried a little chest covered with barnacles.

"They shed their backpacks and snatched off their masks and fins. Scarface tried to open the chest with his bare hands but couldn't. Finally Pogue sent me below for a chisel and hammer. The chest cracked open as soon as he hit the chisel. I held my breath as he dumped the contents on the deck.

"I was excited, but the two men seemed disappointed. Out tumbled half a dozen British coins, and a small packet. Scarface grabbed one of the coins, then began swearing.

" 'The damn thing is dated 1841!' he shouted angrily.

"I realized why the date on the coin was so important. *The ship must have sunk after*

1841, and therefore couldn't be a Spanish galleon carrying gold, for the galleons had sailed past Eleuthera many years before that.

"By now Mr. Pogue had picked up the packet, and was inspecting it. He said the covering was made from a sheep's bladder, which was used during the last century to protect valuable papers at sea. The old man slit open the sheep's bladder with the diving knife and pulled out an envelope with a stamp in one corner. From the envelope he pulled a folded sheet of paper, so old that it crackled.

"It was a short letter. He read it to us." Pim pressed both hands to his forehead. "I can remember it almost word for word. It said, 'My dearest Jeremy, With this letter I send you all my love. It is my hope it reaches you before you sail from Dover. Inasmuch as you are embarked on a half year's voyage to the New World, I hope you will carry this letter with you as a small part of me; as a small reassurance that you carry my love with you; and that you will find me anxiously waiting to be your good wife upon your return, whenever that may be. God keep you safe in His arms. Elizabeth.'

"Scarface started shouting something about the letter being worthless. He was angry at me, and angry at the old man — angry that they'd come all the way to Eleuthera to find a Spanish treasure ship, and instead had found a sailing freighter little more than a hundred years old. He grabbed the coins and shook them in Mr. Pogue's face. 'Some treasure!' he shouted. He said they'd bring a hundred dollars at the most.

"The older man's reply made me like him even more. 'Poor Elizabeth,' he said. 'She never saw Jeremy again. His ship foundered on a coral reef off Eleuthera. I wonder if she waited all her life for him to return.'"

At Pim's feet, Daphne stirred. "That's such a beautiful thought I could cry," she said softly.

Death Comes to Eleuthera

Alvin and Shoie, sitting on the floor with their backs against the wall, were almost lost in the late afternoon shadows of the Swap Shop. "Go on," Alvin urged. "What happened next?"

"I'll never forget the next morning," said Pim. "It was the only morning, since my father gave me the lucky shell, that I forgot to put it in my pocket when I dressed. For some reason I left it on the little table beside my bed. And that day turned out to be the unluckiest day of my life.

"After breakfast I walked over to the harbor and started hosing down the dock.

Thunderheads were building up to the east.

"As I came closer to the *Jennie Bell* I heard voices. After a while the voices grew louder, and then the men started shouting.

"Scarface snarled something about half the money being his, 'even if it was worth only $10,000.' I couldn't understand what he meant, and I still don't.

"The old man said he'd signed Scarface on as a deckhand, and that's exactly the pay that Scarface would get. The boat was his, Mr. Pogue said angrily, and he'd financed every penny of the trip. He was sorry now that he'd paid attention to Scarface when the man came wandering along the dock in Miami, and begged to be taken aboard.

" 'Whatever it sells for, half is mine!' shouted Scarface again.

"Scarface could have the coins, Mr. Pogue offered. They'd be worth more than Scarface had earned, because he'd done no work on the entire trip. Further, Mr. Pogue said, he was wondering about something else. Why had Scarface been so eager to hide on the *Jennie Bell* when it was about to ship out of Miami? Maybe the Miami police would be interested.

" 'I'll kill you!' shouted Scarface.

"Suddenly there was the sound of fighting. It went on for at least sixty seconds, and then the old man opened the cabin door. In two steps he crossed the deck. He stepped up on the rail and leaped to the dock. Scarface was just behind.

" 'Stay out of this, son!' said the old man as he ran past. I saw blood streaming down his shirt.

"Scarface leaped to the dock, and I saw something glittering in his hand. It was the knife that he'd carried, strapped to his leg, the day before.

"Just as Scarface ran past, I flicked the hose. I don't know why I did it. A loop wiggled down the hose, and wrapped itself around Scarface's ankles. He sprawled forward onto his face, and the top of his head struck a mooring cleat. I remember thinking that he must have picked up a lot of splinters in his hands and face. The knife clattered across the dock."

Daphne had been holding her breath. Now she let it out in one long sigh. "Oh, Pim, you're so brave!"

"No," he said thoughtfully. "No, I'm not. I ran. I ran as fast as I could. It wasn't long until I caught up with the old man. He was staggering down the road, his hands clutched to his chest, leaving a trail of blood in the dust.

"I told him I'd guide him to my house. It was slow going. I led him down a shortcut through the brush. I didn't think he'd make it, but he did, and with one final effort he staggered through the door and fell across my bed. He was gasping, and now there was blood trickling down his chin. It came from inside his mouth.

"I grabbed a bucket and ran down the path to the village pump. When I returned, the old man's arms were flung wide apart. One hand rested on my bedside table, the fingers twitching. He was gasping, and I knew he was dying. I told him I'd go get Mrs. Smythe, who does the doctoring until the real doctor can come from Governor's Harbour. Mr. Pogue managed to whisper that it was too late.

"I felt as helpless as I've ever been in my life. I picked up my lucky shell from the table, and rubbed it harder than I'd ever rubbed it before.

"With one finger he beckoned me closer. His lips moved without a sound. Finally he gasped, 'Now you have it. Guard it. Don't let him have it. It's yours now, and I hope — I hope — '

"He never finished the sentence. He trembled once as though he'd had a great chill, and then lay still. I knew he was dead.

"Just then I heard a noise in the doorway. Scarface stood there, his clothes wet and dirty. There were two long scratches down the side of his face, and there was blood in his hair. I knew he'd heard the old man's last words.

"When I saw the knife in his hand I didn't even think. I just turned and jumped through the open window. I ran, and kept running. I know every palmetto and pine in that part of Eleuthera, and I lost Scarface in a hurry.

"Later, I crept back home. I watched the house from a distance for a long time, and saw no sign of Scarface. I figured he was back on the *Jennie Bell*, patching his wounds. I sneaked into the house and left a note for my mother, telling her what had happened. I told her I thought Scarface would continue to watch for me, and that I was going to disappear for a while. I asked her not to worry. Believe me, though, I *was* worried!

"I hid out on the edge of the bonefish flats until dark. Most of the time I was trying to figure out what the 'treasure' was — what Scarface had wanted from the old man, and now wanted from me. The old man hadn't given me a thing, even though he said, 'Now it's yours.' But that didn't count, because *Scarface was convinced I had it*, whatever it was. And he'd already killed to get it.

"Just after sunset the thunderstorm struck. It was the safest time to leave. In the darkness. I stumbled to the harbor and slipped into the warm water, just a little way up the beach from the dock. I could see a light inside the *Jennie Bell*, and a shadow moving across the window.

"Whenever there was a lightning flash, I dived so Scarface couldn't see my head if he was watching. I'm a good swimmer, but I thought I'd never make it. My legs were like lead when finally I grabbed the mooring line of the freighter. I rested a few minutes, then climbed hand over hand up the line. The lightning flashes were constant now, and I had the awful feeling that Scarface was watching me every inch of the way. Finally I fell onto the deck. Because of the storm, no one was about. I found an open hatch, and crept down into the forward hold. There I found some fruit and a few raw vegetables.

"By the time the freighter reached Miami, I promised myself I'd never eat another turnip in my life."

Alvin stood up. Restlessly he moved over to the window and looked out. As he turned around, he asked, "Did you know anybody in Miami?"

"No. At first I didn't even know it was Miami, because I'd never left Eleuthera except for one trip to Nassau when I was five years old.

"All the way from Eleuthera, down in that dark hold, I worried that Scarface had seen me swim out and climb aboard the freighter. If so, he probably had followed the freighter in the *Jennie Bell*, and was after me. I waited until long after dark to slip ashore, then sneaked around the dock area, wondering where I was. Then I began noticing signs: Miami Trucking Company, Miami Harbor Authority, Miami Freight Forwarders.

"I finally found a little park, and slept behind some bushes. I knew I'd have to leave

Miami the next morning, in case Scarface had followed me.

"But the next morning I was too hungry to be careful. I went into a little restaurant on a side street, and asked the man behind the counter if I could work for my breakfast. A tall man sitting on one of the stools looked me over, then asked my name. When I told him, he nodded at the man behind the counter and told him to bring me some orange juice, pancakes, sausage, a couple of eggs, some toast, and a pitcher of milk.

"I've never eaten a meal that tasted as good. The man told me his name was Brian Talley, and asked me what I was doing in Miami. His way of talking sounded a little strange to me, so I knew *my* way of talking must sound strange to *him*.

"I made up a story as I went along. I said I was from Nassau, where I'd lived with my sister who died two weeks before. Now I was trying to get to my brother's house. He lived in Chicago, I said, which was the first city that popped into my mind, even though I didn't know where it was. I told Brian Talley that some sport fishermen had brought me from Nassau to Miami.

"My lucky shell was really working for

me that day. Brian was a truck driver. He was leaving for Des Moines by way of Chicago as soon as the truck was loaded. He said he'd take me along. He told me to get my duds.

Pim laughed a little, almost to himself. "I didn't understand what duds meant. When he told me, I didn't have anything except what I was wearing. He took me down the street to a store, where he bought me a little canvas bag, two pairs of shorts, an extra shirt, some socks, and a pair of sneakers. He made me wear the shoes, even though I hated the feel of them. I never wear them on Eleuthera. And he put a five-dollar bill in my pocket. Said I should have it, just in case I'd ever want an extra hamburger somewhere, and he wasn't around. Brian Talley is a very nice man.

"He had a huge truck. I guess you call it a semi. It seemed like I climbed a hundred feet to get up into the cab beside Brian, but I was very proud and happy to be there. He started the big engine, and we rolled out along the highway. Did you ever know how many gears there are in a big truck? It seemed like Brian was shifting forever.

"I didn't realize it until too late, but our

route led right past the Miami dock area. I'd been watching Brian steer through the city traffic, when I happened to glance out the window. I froze. There, tied up at the dock, was the *Jennie Bell*. And just stepping ashore was Scarface! He looked up. Our eyes locked for a moment, and then I dropped to the floor of the cab.

"When Brian asked me what was wrong, I just crouched there and shivered for a minute, then made up the story that I'd dropped something on the floor. I didn't want to get him involved in my problems.

"After a while, I got to feeling a little better. What could Scarface do, with Brian around? Anyway, we'd probably left Scarface back in Miami.

"Brian showed me how to operate the citizen-band radio inside the cab. It's a lot like marine radios, which I've listened to for years, but the truck drivers speak a different language. Brian taught it to me. For example, the first time he picked up the microphone and switched it on, he said something like:

'This is Juice Loader B.T. rolling north on the nine-five toward Windy

City. Longside is my new little partner, the Bahamas Kid. He's getting his first look at the States, so hey out there, Good Buddy, holler a hello toward him. And if you see any Bears up ahead, I'd appreciate a shout. Ten-four.'

"Brian taught me that what he'd said, when he was talking into the microphone like that, was something like:

'Hello, anybody who can hear, this is Brian Talley driving a load of oranges north on Highway 95 toward Chicago. Beside me is a boy I call the Bahamas Kid. He's never been in the United States before, so greet him over the radio. And if you see any highway patrolmen up ahead, I'd appreciate it if you'd let me know.'

"Then, over the radio, would come some kind of answer like:

'Hey Juice Loader B.T., I'm out ahead and can watch your front door for you. Tell that Bahamas Kid to have a bright day, and mobile safe. This is the Big Wheez.'

"Of course what he meant was that he'd watch for patrolmen ahead of us, and to say hello to the Bahamas Kid.

"We had a lot of fun on the radio, joking back and forth with the other drivers. I became known as the *Bahamas Kid*. We also had a lot of fun talking to each other. Brian said he liked my lingo, as he called it, so I told him Bahamian stories my mother had taught me. I learned to like hamburgers, and hot dogs, and I even tried steak once. It was good, but I'd rather have red snapper with rice.

"Then Brian said it was our last day before we arrived in Chicago. He joked over the radio with a couple of other drivers about me, and about the traffic up ahead, then stopped here in Riverton for a cup of coffee. I had a Coke, and was looking out the window of the little restaurant when I saw a blue car go by, with a big antenna towering above it. I knew by now that the antenna was the sign of a C-B radio. At the same time, I saw the driver. Scarface.

"Suddenly I knew how Scarface had followed me. Everytime Brian had sent out a radio message, he'd mentioned the Bahamas Kid, and also our location. It was easy for anyone to follow us.

"At the same time, I realized that my only chance of losing Scarface was to get away from Brian and his radio — much as I hated the idea. I told Brian I wanted to get some fresh air while he finished his coffee. Outside the restaurant, I hid behind a big sign, beside Brian's truck. I could see just a bit, between the boards.

"Finally Brian came out and looked in the cab for me. He searched around, looking up and down the highway. Then he just climbed into the truck and waited. He must have waited three or four hours. Finally I heard the click as he jerked the C-B microphone out of its holder. Then I heard his clear, strong voice:

'Breaker One-Nine! This is Juice Loader B.T. heading toward Windy City northbound on six-five, just leaving Riverton, Indiana. I've lost my little partner, the Bahamas Kid. He's about eleven years old, dark complexion, and blond hair. I'll give bucks to anyone who can transmit info on him. Contact Juice Loader B.T. at Braden Trucking in Windy City, or give me a shout along the way. Juice Loader signing off. We're clear.'

"He started the big truck engine, and rolled slowly away. I cried a little, behind that signboard. Brian is a fine man.

"But without knowing it, he'd just done the worst thing he possibly could do. He'd told Scarface, over the radio, that I was staying behind in Riverton.

"That night I found a deserted farmhouse out on the edge of your town. The garden there still has a few carrots and some onions in it. That's what I've had to eat."

Disaster!

It took all of Alvin's powers of persuasion to convince Pim that, for his own good, he should have some more of Mom Fernald's food, and then sleep through the night in the Swap Shop.

"You'll be safer here than wandering the streets," Alvin pointed out. "I promise for your mother's sake that we won't go to the police — at least not just yet. And who knows, maybe Scarface will have given up his search by tomorrow morning. Anyway, Pim, I'll come up with some kind of solution to your problem by breakfast time tomorrow."

"Yeah. And you can rely on the Magnificent Brain," pointed out Shoie.

"*Please* stay," was all Daphne could say.

"We'll be back soon with some food," explained Alvin. "Then we'll lock you in the Swap Shop for the night."

When Alvin and Daphne arrived home, dinner was almost ready. "Instead of eating here, can Alvin and Shoie and I have a picnic?" begged Daphne, glancing at Alvin for guidance.

"It's too late for that," Mom said. "Dinner's almost on the table."

"Pleeeeeeeeeeeaaaze, Mom."

"It's such great weather out," chimed in Alvin.

"Well. Well, if it's all right with your father, it's all right with me."

Minutes later, Alvin was carving three big chunks out of the meat loaf while Pest packed bread, potato chips, apples, and paper plates in a picnic basket.

At the last minute Alvin ran upstairs and returned with two old blankets from the closet.

"Seems to me one blanket would be enough for a picnic," sniffed Mom disapprovingly. Then she added, "Besides you kids left very little meat loaf for your father and me. You must be planning to feed an army."

"I'm hungry, Mom," said Alvin truthfully.

"Well, you'd better put some cookies in. And there's some leftover potato salad in the refrigerator."

The kids picked up Shoie, then trooped down the street to the Swap Shop. The door was locked from inside, and they had to identify themselves repeatedly before Pim opened the door, a fearful look on his face.

Half an hour later Pim was feeling much better.

"Meat loaf does that to me too," announced the Pest.

"What?" asked Pim.

"Feels me better."

"Oh."

Alvin said, "We don't have to go home for another hour, Pim. Tell us more about Eleuthera. Forget all about Scarface. Just tell us about your island."

They listened, entranced, as Pim described island life. He told them all about diving among the coral heads, in the strangely silent but beautiful world beneath the surface. He talked about the fish that inhabited the water — the gorgeous red snapper, the graceful French angelfish, the hundred-pound grouper, and the baleful barracuda. He told them which sharks were dangerous, and which were no more harmful than a goldfish. He talked about his friends, black and white, who lived in Gregory Town. He told them about the little pink building that was his favorite spot on earth — his school, and how there were very few textbooks for each class.

Time passed quickly. When Alvin announced that they had to go home, Daphne spread the blankets over the flour sacks to make a softer bed for Pim.

It was twilight when they slipped out the front door of the Swap Shop. "Don't forget to lock the door after us," whispered Alvin.

There was no need for the reminder. Almost as soon as he'd spoken the words, Alvin heard the click of the lock.

Alvin didn't sleep well that night. Once he awoke with such a shout that Mom came running into his room to see what was wrong. She held him tightly for four or five minutes, which she hadn't done for years; it was the best feeling he'd had in a long time.

In the morning, when he awoke from his troubled sleep, he had a sense of disaster.

"I have to get to the Swap Shop right away," he told Mom. He swallowed a glass of milk, picked up a sweet roll, and was out the door and onto his bike before she could reply. The Pest was at his heels, still rubbing her eyes.

Shoie was waiting on his front stoop. He, too, looked troubled. "I wonder if Pim is all right," he said softly as he swung aboard his bike.

Alvin knew that his feeling had been right as soon as he rounded the corner and got his first look at the Swap Shop.

The door was standing wide open.

A tornado had hit the inside. Stock was strewn everywhere. Hoses and garden tools, bicycle fenders and hats had been trampled on the floor. Dishes and glasses were lying in shattered layers. Buckets of paint had been opened and hurled against the wall. The flour sacks had been heaved about the room.

Alvin walked over to the corner, and picked up two blankets they'd brought the evening before. Their hems had been savagely ripped apart. He found Pim's little bag; every seam had been torn open. Pim's spare shirt and underwear were in ribbons.

Daphne started to cry softly.

Alvin stood in the middle of the room, Pim's bag in his arms. Finally he said quietly, "We've got to keep our heads. We can't panic now, *we've got to keep our heads and think this out!*"

"If we ever needed the Magnificent Brain, we need it now, old man," said Shoie.

"I'll tell you something good, right off the bat, without thinking much about it," said Alvin. "I think Pim is all right. I don't think he's hurt. And I think he's still around somewhere."

"How can you say that, Alvin?" sniffled Daphne. "How can you say he's all right when you see all this mess?"

"Use your head. The Swap Shop has been searched from bottom to top. Even the clothing and blankets have been ripped apart. Now ask yourself, why did Scarface make such a complete search? If Pim were still here, he would have taken what he wanted from Pim. It seems to me that proves that Pim wasn't here. Besides, look at the back window." It was wide open. "I figure Pim heard Scarface trying to force the front door. He went to the back window, quietly opened it, and slipped out. That left Scarface inside an empty room when he finally broke the lock. But how could he *know for sure* that Pim still had the treasure? Perhaps Pim, in his hurry to escape, left it behind. The treasure Scarface is searching for, if it exists at all, obviously is worth a great deal of money, and Scarface can't take a chance on missing it anywhere. He had no idea where Pim had gone, so he did the best thing he could think of — at least from his standpoint. He searched the Swap Shop to make absolutely sure the treasure wasn't still here."

Daphne had stopped sniffling. "Oh, Alvin, you think so *hard* and so *good* sometimes."

"So what's our next move, old bean?" asked Shoie.

"I want to think this through a little further," said Alvin. "Let the Magnificent Brain noodle it around for a while. Tell you what. If you kids don't mind, I wish you'd start cleaning up this mess while I put the ol' Brain into action."

"Ol' Brain into action," echoed the Pest.

"Good idea," agreed Shoie.

An hour later, Shoie and Daphne walked out into the sunshine. Alvin was sitting on the front step.

"Well, we threw out all the broken stuff, and sorted out everything that's good," said Shoie. "I think we're back in business again."

Alvin was tugging on his left ear. The Magnificent Brain was in high gear.

"Shhhhhh!" said the Pest reverently. She and Shoie sat down beside Alvin.

The motion seemed to rouse him. He looked up, and his eyes seemed to swim back into focus. "How are things inside?" he asked.

"Alvin, you don't hear *anything* while you're thinking. Do you?"

"I was just thinking," he said, as though she hadn't even spoken. "I was just thinking. One question lies at the heart of this whole mystery — and possibly it's the key to Pim's safety."

"What question?" asked his sister.

"*Who* is Scarface?"

"What difference does that make?" asked Shoie.

"If we can learn his identity, we may not only learn how to deal with him, but we may find the answer to the other question."

"What's the other question?"

"Exactly what is the treasure?" Alvin

slipped into a formal way of speaking — as though he were in a lecture hall. "We can deduce the treasure is quite small — Scarface ripped apart the hems of the blankets, smashed small vases, and obviously searched every cranny of the Swap Shop. I'll admit I don't know what the treasure is, but it has to be small, and it probably still is hidden somewhere. We can't be *sure* Scarface didn't find it in the Swap Shop, but I have a strong hunch that he didn't. The treasure may still be in Eleuthera. Pim says he doesn't have any idea what it is. Therefore he couldn't hide it. Therefore Scarface couldn't find it."

"Good thinking, old man!" exclaimed Shoie.

"Thanks, old bean," responded Alvin.

"So what's the next move?"

"The next move," announced the Pest with great determination, standing up, "is to find Pim. That's the most important of all."

"You're right, Sis," said Alvin quietly. "You're right. That's most important of all. Except that we have no idea where he is. No more idea than Scarface has."

He waited for her to respond. Moments

later she said, "Well. Well. Well, I guess you're right."

"We have to wait for *him* to contact *us*," Alvin said. "And I really believe he will. It may be hours, or even days from now, but sooner or later I'm sure Pim will come to us again. Meanwhile, we should keep trying to help him by solving other problems."

"Like what, old bean?" It was Shoie, of course.

"Like what I said at first. Let's find out *who Scarface is*."

"How do we do that?"

"We try to identify Scarface in the police files. Through a photograph."

"But Alvin, we don't have a picture of him," wailed Daphne.

"We can. We can have a photograph of him in just a few minutes, once we find him. We can take it with a Polaroid camera."

"But we don't have a Polaroid camera."

Alvin held up one finger. "Ah. That's where the Swap Shop comes in. Beetle Larson has a Polaroid. Beetle wants a guitar. Milly Pelcher has a guitar she no longer is interested in. Milly is interested in anything that will impress people. A merry-go-round horse will impress people. Do I make myself clear?"

"*Very* clear," said Shoie. "And I think I'm the one who has to carry the horse over to Milly's house." He flexed his mightly muscles.

Scarface Poses
for a Picture

The kids locked up the Swap Shop and rode their bikes out South Main Street toward the highway.

Slantwise across Alvin's shoulder was slung Beetle Larson's Polaroid. At least it *had* been Beetle's Polaroid ten minutes before. Actually, the swapping had gone fast. Shoie and Alvin had struggled over to Milly's house with the merry-go-round horse. She had fallen in love with it at once, and told them to place it in her room at the foot of her bed. They'd raced away with her guitar, which she hadn't touched for more than a year, and pulled up breathlessly in front of the Larson home.

Beetle himself was lying on a big branch of a huge oak tree in his front yard. He did this often — so often that the bark was all worn off. Once, in the heat of the summer sun, he'd fallen asleep and slipped out of the tree. He had seven stitches in his right ear.

In any case, Alvin found Beetle in the tree, and almost instantly persuaded him to swap his five-year-old camera for the guitar. Beetle fancied himself a country and western singer, and wanted to learn the guitar so he could wear glittery clothes and make as much money as Glen Campbell. Quickly he showed Alvin how to use the camera.

As the kids were leaving, they saw Beetle tie a rope to the guitar, climb the tree holding the other end of the rope, carefully pull the guitar up after him, then sit down on his limb and clasp the guitar to his chest.

"*Oh, the highway is lonely from Nashville,*" he shouted in a falsetto voice, twanging the guitar strings as though he knew what he was doing, "*and my true love is no longer true . . .*"

They approached the Sleep Snug Motel cautiously from a side street. It occurred to Alvin, as they swung off their bikes and parked them in a vacant lot, that Scarface just *might* have captured Pim. In fact, Pim might be inside the motel right now. Alvin had a mental picture of Pim, bound and gagged, lying on a bed with Scarface standing over him trying to learn the whereabouts of the treasure — whatever it was.

Cautiously they walked half a block along the side of the motel, then peered around the corner. Parked in front of one unit was the same green car that Scarface had been driving. He was still there!

At that instant one of the motel doors opened and Scarface came striding out. He squinted up at the sky, as though checking the weather. He yawned, and reached into his pocket. Alvin jerked the camera off his shoulder, and raised the viewfinder to his eye. He focused it, and put his finger on the shutter release. Scarface's face was hidden momentarily, then he turned to unlock the car door. Alvin snapped the shutter.

He forgot that if the camera could see Scarface, Scarface could see the camera.

"Hey!"

"Run!" shouted Alvin.

"Run!" echoed Daphne, already ten steps ahead of the other two kids.

Daphne was the fastest starter, and Shoie

was the fastest runner, so it was Alvin who kept falling behind. Once when he looked back over his shoulder he saw Scarface surprisingly close.

It was one of the closest calls Alvin ever had. He reached his bike, slung the camera over the handlebars, and swung up onto the seat. Daphne and Shoie already were half a block down the street.

"Wait!" shouted Scarface, now only a few yards from the bike. "Wait! I won't hurt you!"

Alvin stood up on his pedals. The rear wheel slewed dangerously to one side, but Alvin kept his balance. He gained speed, but by now he could hear Scarface puffing just behind. There was one agonizing moment when the bike gave a terrible shudder. Alvin knew Scarface had reached for the back fender and managed to jar it, but hadn't been able to grab hold.

Then Alvin was pulling steadily away.

"I'll fix you!" shouted Scarface, standing in the middle of the street. "I'll fix you, and when I do, you'll wish you'd never seen me!"

I already wish that, thought Alvin.

The two other kids slowed their pace, and Alvin caught up. He wheeled down the alley between Second and Third streets, and skidded to a stop behind Mrs. Johnson's garage.

"Let's wait here for a few minutes," Alvin said. "That guy scares me to death, and by now he's probably in his car looking for us."

"And for Pim," Daphne said in a small voice.

Alvin unstrapped the camera from the handlebars. He operated all the controls exactly as Beetle had shown him. Finally he peeled back the piece of heavy photo paper. On the other side was a remarkably clear photo of Scarface looking directly into the camera lens.

"Our next big problem," said Alvin, "is to see if we can identify this photo at police headquarters."

"Why is that such a problem?" asked Daphne. "Can't we just show it to Dad, or one of the other officers?" She and Alvin knew every policeman in town, thanks to Dad's position as a police sergeant.

"No, we can't. Remember, I promised Pim I wouldn't say a thing about this yet, to protect his mother. I'm going to keep that promise."

"Then I don't see how we can possibly identify the photo," said Shoie.

A moment of silence. Daphne said softly,

but with great confidence, "I can do it. I know I can. Just let me have the picture, Alvin."

He looked at her in surprise. "What're you planning to do, Sis?"

"Never mind. I can do it. Just give me the picture." Then she added, as an afterthought, "Is there any chocolate cake left at home, Alvin?"

He exploded. "Oh, c'mon, Pest. You can't be thinking about your stomach at a time like this!"

"I'm not. I'm thinking of someone else's stomach. Give me the picture, Alvin. I'll stop at home, and see about the chocolate cake myself."

Never had Alvin seen her so determined. Perhaps it was the fact that Pim was missing. Anyway, there was something in her tone of voice that made him surrender the photograph. "Don't take any chances, Sis. Scarface is probably riding around looking for us. Take the alleys and side streets. If he should see you, just run to the first open door you see. Don't even knock. Just run on in, and call the police."

"Okay," she said in a small voice.

He put his hands on her shoulders. "Just identify Scarface."

"For Pim?"

"Yes, for Pim."

Without another word she rode off down the alley.

"We'll meet you back at the Swap Shop," he called.

Daphne Tries
Some Flattery

The big plate-glass door at the police station was almost too heavy. Daphne tugged with one hand — the other held a paper sack — until the door was open about a foot. Then she slipped through and at the same time let loose of the handle. She wasn't quite fast enough; the door swung around and caught her by one arm and one leg. She was trapped.

Daphne looked around the station. Dad was probably out in one of the police cars. Seated behind the duty desk was Sergeant Ellsworth, busily working on some printed forms.

"Ow," Daphne said softly.

Sergeant Ellsworth looked up. He was a tall, thin man with bushy gray eyebrows that waggled when he talked. A smile of welcome crossed his face. "Hi, Daphne!"

"Could you help me, Sergeant Ellsworth? Ow."

"Ow, what? Oh, I see. You're trapped in the door. Here, let me give you a hand."

He came around the desk and held the door for her, with a little bow. "Looking for your dad? I'm afraid he's on duty in one of the patrol cars until noon. Why don't you come back then?"

"No, I'm not looking for Daddy." Daphne paused a moment. She hadn't known who would be behind the desk, but Sergeant Ellsworth was perfect for her plan. She gave him her most flirtatious smile. "Actually, I was looking for *you*."

"For me, is it?" His eyebrows waggled. "Now, what would a pretty little girl like you want with me?"

"Well, you see, I thought of you right away when I woke up after my bad dream last night. It was a horrible dream, a real nightmare, and you saved me from the bad guy."

"So you have nightmares about me, eh?"

"No. You know what I mean. You *saved* me. So this morning I thought to myself it would be nice to give that wonderful Sergeant Ellsworth a piece of homemade chocolate cake for being so nice to me in my dream. That's why I'm here." She put the paper sack on the desk. "Here's the cake. I helped Mom make it myself."

"Well now, Daphne, that's mighty thoughtful of you." He peeked inside the sack. "Uuummmmmm! Looks scrumptious. I really am mighty proud to be in your dreams, Daphne."

"Mighty glad to have you there, Sergeant Ellsworth."

"What did I save you from?"

"A horrible criminal. He had an ugly face, with a scar running down one side of it, and he kept chasing me, and chasing me, and chasing me." She gave him a calculating glance. "And my dream made me wonder how you identify a criminal that you've seen. I got to wondering real hard about it. And since you were in my dream, I decided to ask you to explain it to me this morning, when I brought you that piece of cake I helped make myself."

"Well, I guess I could show one of the

finest little citizens of our city how we do that. C'mon into the records room, Daphne."

He led the way into a long, narrow room that was filled with row after row of shelves.

"Mostly these are records of our own work here in Riverton," he explained with a wave of his hand. "But you don't want to see these records. Sit down at the desk over there."

He disappeared among the shelves. When he returned he was carrying a heavy, cloth-bound book.

"Here you are." He placed the book on the desk in front of her. "We call this our mugbook." He flipped through the book at random. The pages were covered with photos. "All criminals," he said.

"What a lot of them!" exclaimed Daphne. "And some don't even look like criminals."

"There's no special 'criminal look,' Daphne. I've known criminals who look just as distinguished as Supreme Court justices."

"This is all so interesting, Sergeant Ells-worth. How do you use these books?"

"If you've seen the criminal— as you did in your dream— then you just keep looking until you find his picture. Beneath the picture is all the information that the police departments and the FBI have on the man — aliases, age, prior record, addresses, everything. But I don't really think" — the eyebrows waggled — "you'll find the man of your dreams, Daphne. After all, he *was* in your dreams."

"I know. But he was so *real*." She pretended to shudder. "Anyway, do you mind if I look through here for a few minutes?"

"Not at all. I have to get back to the desk. Call me when you're through."

She gave him her sweetest smile. Gravely he saluted, did a military about-face, and marched out the door.

She didn't have much time; he might grow suspicious. She opened the book at page one and looked at the men gazing straight up at her. Beneath two photos she caught the word "Murder." This time her shudder was real.

She started slowly, too slowly. Soon she found she could gain speed by paying no attention to the pictures themselves; she looked only for a face with a long livid scar.

Fifteen minutes passed, then twenty. Her arms were tired from turning the pages, her eyes were tired from the search. And still she was little more than halfway through the book.

When she spotted Scarface she was so

surprised that she gave out a little shriek, then quickly covered her mouth. There was no question about it. Scarface gazed straight out at her, a scowl frozen on his face. Down his right cheek ran a livid white scar.

Or was it him, after all? The man in the photo had extremely short hair. And it seemed to her that perhaps his face was a little fuller than Scarface's, the cheeks a little fatter, the lower lip a little larger.

She fumbled through the pocket of her jeans. Out came the Polaroid shot they had taken less than an hour before. She placed it beside the mug shot and bent over to inspect it closely. The two faces looked very similar, but the lighting was different. She couldn't be quite sure.

The scar, she suddenly realized, would be *definite* proof one way or the other. No two scars are exactly alike, Dad had once explained to her, which is why they frequently are used for identification. Slowly she traced the scar in its zigzag course down the cheek in the mug shot, then in the Polaroid.

It was Scarface. No question about it.

Daphne opened the center drawer of the desk. She took out a sheet of paper and the stub of a pencil. As quickly as she could, she copied off all the information beneath the photo. She folded the paper around the Polaroid shot, and slipped both in her pocket.

"I'm through, Sergeant Ellsworth," she called. Then, to keep him under her spell, she said brightly as he came through the door, "Everybody says I make the best fudge in town. I'd like to bring you a batch sometime soon for being nice to me — and for saving me in my dream."

Sergeant Ellsworth's eyebrows waggled more furiously than ever.

A Conference in the
Swap Shop

When Alvin and Shoie wheeled up to the
Swap Shop, Alvin was in a foul mood. Re-
gardless of his hopeful words to Daphne and
Shoie, it was quite possible that Pim had
been captured, even killed, because Alvin
had insisted he stay overnight. Scarface had
killed once before, and it was obvious he'd
stop at nothing to get his hands on the treasure he believed was in Pim's possession.

Alvin unlocked the Swap Shop and angrily
flung open the door. For a moment he
couldn't believe his eyes.

There was Pim!

The boy was as startled as Alvin, and

made a leap toward the window, before he realized who was standing in the doorway. He let out a long sigh, then said with deep feeling, "I'm so glad it's you!" Pim's hair was mussed and his eyes were swollen, as though he'd had no sleep. "I would thank you if you'd close the door, Alvin. He must be somewhere close on my trail."

Alvin closed the door. "He is. Stay back from the window, Pim."

Alvin sat down on the floor in the middle of the Swap Shop, and the other two kids followed suit. "Tell us what happened last night, Pim. We hoped that you'd escaped, but we couldn't be sure."

"Indeed I escaped, but barely. In the middle of the night I awoke, and heard a scraping sound at the front door. As quietly as I could I got to my feet and eased open the window. There was a rattling in the door lock, and I knew that someone — Scarface, of course — was trying to pick the lock. I climbed over the windowsill and dropped to the ground just as I heard the door swing open. I sneaked around to the side of the building, and could hear him swearing in a whisper as he looked around the room. Then he started tearing things apart." Pim paused. "I'm so sorry I brought all this trouble to you."

"Don't worry, Pim. We *like* helping you. Where did you stay last night?"

"I hid under a bench in the park. Then, as soon as your library was open, I went inside and read books. The librarian looked at me a trifle strangely, but I didn't care. Alvin, you must have the most beautiful library in the world. Thousands and thousands of books! If only we had such a library on Eleuthera."

"Maybe you will someday," said Shoie cheerfully.

"Why did you come back to the Swap Shop?" asked Alvin.

"Only to get my things." Pim pointed to his little bag beside the window. "But they aren't even worth taking along. He ruined everything. Now I must leave. Every minute I am here, I put you in danger. Please forgive me, and accept my thanks for everything you've done. I'll take a roundabout way out of town, and get away before Scarface sees me."

"Wait!" ordered Alvin. He leaned his back against Mr. Barclay's treadmill. "Just a minute. Let's analyze this problem carefully."

"Alvin's Magnificent Brain," Shoie explained to Pim, "works like a computer. All he has to do is switch it on."

"I see," said Pim, though there was a doubtful look on his face.

For half an hour Alvin sat there, unblinking, staring into space. Finally his hand moved up to his right earlobe and began tugging on it. "Let's look at it this way," he said suddenly. "Suppose you run away again, Pim. There's no telling *for sure* whether Scarface will spot you before you leave town. You have very little money, so you'll have to depend on hitching a ride with someone. Scarface will be cruising along both main highways, one after the other, again and again, in hopes of spotting you. And even if you manage to get away, you'll never be sure that he won't find you, somewhere, some other time. You can't go home. That's what he'll expect you to do. You'll be looking over your shoulder the rest of your life. And you'll never know what's happened to your mother. That's no way to live, Pim."

"But what other choice do I have?"

Alvin never had a chance to answer. At that moment the front door burst open and the Pest danced in. When she saw Pim her mouth flew open. She ran to him and hugged him quickly. Then, her cheeks bright red, she took a couple of steps backward.

"I'm so glad to see you," she said.

"I'm very glad to see you again too," he replied gravely.

"Hey, Pest, what did you find out?" Alvin broke in.

She whirled around once, then sat down on the floor. "I found out *all* about him." Daphne put on her "official" face. She pronounced her words very clearly, and spoke as though she had done most of the police work herself. "We identified Scarface without any trouble by comparing his photograph to what we call mug shots. These are photographs of known criminals that are distributed to police departments throughout the country."

She dug into her pocket and pulled out a slip of paper. "The mug shots prove that Scarface's real name is David Wasco. He also goes under aliases — that means just-pretend names — of Douglas Watley and Gary Warren. He has twice been convicted of assault, and was arrested two months ago for attempting to smuggle narcotics into Florida. He escaped from the Dade County

Jail while awaiting trial on the smuggling charge. He is probably armed and considered dangerous. Approach with caution." She looked around at the other kids. "So there!"

"Great work, Sis!" said Alvin.

"How did you get all that information?" asked Shoie in amazement.

"No wonder he wanted to ship out with Mr. Pogue," said Pim thoughtfully. "He was running from the police."

There was a long silence.

Finally Pim said, "Probably armed."

"Extremely dangerous," said Shoie.

"Approach with caution," said Daphne.

The Magnificent Brain Comes Up with a Plan

"Wait just a minute," said Alvin. "I want to run this problem through a new circuit."

The kids sat on the floor watching Alvin, who seemed hypnotized. He fixed his gaze unwaveringly on an Easter egg basket hanging against the far wall. His forehead was scrunched into deep wrinkles.

Finally the Pest could stand it no longer. "You all right, Alvin?"

Alvin's eyes blinked and he shifted his gaze around the room. As he did so, a remarkable thing happened. He seemed to see each item — the used fire hose, the cowboy hats, the boxes of feathers, the Halloween

125

masks, in a new light. There was a brilliant flash inside the Magnificent Brain.

Alvin started talking rapidly. "I have analyzed this situation thoroughly and come up with the only possible solution. Pim, I already have proved that you no longer can run from Scarface. If you do, you'll be running the rest of your life. He might never find you again, but you won't *know* that he can't find you. No, you must stay here in Riverton. We must solve the problem here and now.

"By now, Scarface may have given up. But I don't think so. I really don't think so. The treasure — whatever it is — is so valuable it has become an obsession with him. He has killed one man for it, and chased Pim across ocean waters and halfway across the United States. No, I think he'll make one more great effort to get his hands on the treasure."

"I'd give it to him," said Pim quietly, "if I had it."

"Actually, we're now in a position where *we don't want Scarface to leave*. If he disappears now, Pim will never know when he'll reappear. And Pim's mother is in danger too. *So we must do everything we can* to keep Scarface right here in Riverton until we learn the secret of the treasure. Even if he was arrested for smuggling and sent to prison, Pim couldn't be sure he wouldn't show up years from now, after he'd been released." Alvin's voice suddenly grew solemn. "Kids, from this moment on we have four goals. First, we must keep Scarface in Riverton. Second, we must capture him. Third, we must solve the mystery of the treasure. And fourth, we must find the treasure, if it exists, and *dispose of it forever*, in front of Scarface, and in such a final way that he'll know he no longer can hope to get his hands on it even after he's released from prison for smuggling and for murder. *Those are the things we must do if Pim is to be safe.*"

"*Capture* Scarface?" Shoie's Adam's apple bounded up and down as he swallowed.

"*Find* the treasure?" Pim looked at Alvin as though he were mad.

"*Give away* the treasure?" It was Daphne's small voice. "How are we going to do all those things, Alvin? Just tell me. How are we going to do all of those things?"

Alvin's eyes were gazing at the Easter basket, but in reality were focused on the

TV screen inside the Magnificent Brain. "I have an idea how we can achieve all four of our goals. There are still some problems to be worked out, but none is insoluble. My idea is based upon what I call the Law of Predictability."

"The law of *what*?" asked Shoie.

"The Law of Predictability. For example —" he placed his foot on Tubby's creeper, which was nearby —"if I push this with my foot, it will slide across the room until it strikes something and stops." He gave it a push. It rolled to the far wall and came to a stop. "If you know enough about an object, you can predict exactly what it will do under any circumstance. *And the same thing is true of human beings. If you know enough about them, you can predict their actions too.*"

"What's this got to do with Scarface?" asked Daphne.

"If we use predictable things to put Scarface into a situation which we design ourselves, then his behavior will be predictable. It's the Law of Predictability."

Shoie said, "I don't understand, but if the Magnificent Brain says so, then I believe, brother, I believe. What things do we need?"

"We need a lot of stuff from here in the Swap Shop — the stuffed owl, that window fan we got from Mrs. Nardulli, the treadmill, the old amplifier and speakers from the skating rink, Mr. Ginzburg's spotlights, Tubby's creeper. We'll all need dark glasses and those earmuffs we got from Wart van Wert. Oh, yes — we'll need Jennie Oostermeyer's feathers. I knew those would come in handy some day. Now listen close and I'll tell you what we'll do with all that stuff. First we'll have to —"

His voice droned on and on. At first the others looked at him as though he were mad. Gradually, though, he hypnotized them by showing them how *predictable* everything was.

His plan might work, the others thought. It just might work. And the other three kids began offering suggestions themselves.

Alvin's clincher came when he reached the end of his plan. Without any warning he said, "Also, I think I know *where* we'll find the treasure — and *what it is.*"

The Capture!

"Ooogggle obdie smorzen!"

"What did you say, Daphne?" Alvin whispered.

"Oooggle obdie smorzen!"

Alvin took a chance on speaking aloud. "Doggone it, Pest, take off those earmuffs so you can hear me. Now what did you say?"

"I say it's hard to hear and talk with earmuffs on. Besides, I can't see anything through these dark glasses."

"Well, put them back on. You're going to need them soon. I hope."

"I'm beginning to hope *not*," whispered Shoie from a far corner. "I don't mind telling you I'm scared, Alvin. This is a pretty crazy scheme. Maybe it won't work. Then what'll we do?"

The light was so dim in the Swap Shop — coming through the window from the street-light outside — that Alvin could scarcely see the other kids through his dark glasses. He, Daphne, and Shoie were each hidden in the deep shadows of different corners of the big room. Each wore a pair of the old earmuffs they'd acquired from Wart van Wert, and a pair of dark glasses contributed to the Swap Shop by old Doc Seymour, although right now the earmuffs were off their ears and the dark glasses perched on top of their heads.

Pim was standing as rigid as a sentry in front of the door, which was closed and latched from the inside.

"I agree with Shoie," Pim's voice trembled slightly as he spoke. "Perhaps your plan won't work. Perhaps someone will be hurt. I think it best that we all leave this place."

"My plan will work." Alvin emphasized each word. He tried to make it sound absolutely certain — as though there was not a doubt in his mind about the outcome. But inside his chest was a big black ball of fear that he couldn't completely cover up.

131

"All right," whispered Pim. "I have faith in you, my friend. And you are right when you say that I can't hide for the rest of my life. As long as that man is free, I'll always be worried for my mother and for myself. My regret is that I am endangering your lives. He will do anything to find that treasure, whatever it is. Perhaps Daphne, at least, should leave."

"Not on your life!" This time Daphne had no trouble hearing Pim's words. "If you guys go through with this, so will I. Besides, if I left, who'd operate the stuffed owl?"

"Okay, we'll work it just as planned," said Alvin, the authority rising in his voice. "Let's go down our checklist once more. How about the spotlights, Shoie?"

"Got my hand on the switch right now. Hope I don't blow a fuse."

"Okay. Is the treadmill exactly where we want it, Pim?"

"Righto."

"Good. And I have the treadmill control box here. What about your stuff, Daphne?"

"The owl's hanging on the edge of the shelf. You hooked up the tape recorder, amplifier, and speaker yourself, Alvin, so you already know about them. And I have that pull-chain you gave me right here. I'm ready to pull it anytime you say."

"Check. Shoie, how about you?"

"Engine oil ready. And Tubby's creeper is right beside the treadmill."

"Okay. Everybody got their earmuffs and dark glasses ready?"

Mumbled agreement came from the corners of the room.

Alvin took a deep breath. Tension was building inside the Swap Shop. "Okay, gang," he said, his whisper pitched a little higher than normal. "I'll bet Scarface is out there right now, watching for any sign of Pim. Let's see if we can hook our fish." For some reason he found it difficult to talk. He swallowed twice, even though his mouth was dry. Finally he spoke the words that were to commit them to perhaps the greatest danger of their lives. "Okay, Pim. Go on out. But be sure you stay close to the door. You're the bait, but we don't want anything to happen to you."

There was a moment of silence, then the door swung open. For a brief second Alvin glimpsed a rectangle of light, with Pim's silhouette in the center. Then Pim slipped through the doorway and vanished.

Alvin's heart was thumping so loud it sounded like the big bass drum in the high school band. He was short of breath, and sweat ran down inside the dark glasses, stinging his eyes.

The door was still partially open, admitting a little light. He glanced across at the dim figure of his sister. It seemed to him that her face had turned totally white. The dark glasses gave her the appearance of a great white owl, to match the owl just above her head.

Slowly Alvin swiveled his neck around until he could see Shoie. Good ol' Shoe. He's probably scared to death, just as I am, but he's always ready to do anything the Magnificent Brain dreams up. Nobody could ask for a better pal. Someday I'm going to —

"EEEEEEYYYOOOOOOWWW!"

The door burst open so suddenly that it slammed back against the wall. There was a tinkling sound as the glass insert broke.

Pim dashed blindly into the darkened room. He had rehearsed his next move many times, but now his knees were shaking so violently he could hardly keep his feet. He managed to stagger straight down the path that the kids had cleared through all the

Swap Shop junk. He tripped over the front edge of the treadmill, regained his balance, ran up the slight incline, and jumped off the far side.

As he whirled around, a man's figure appeared in the doorway.

"*Scarface!*" thought the Pest in panic. *Run!* Instead, she shrank back into the corner.

Scarface! thought Shoie. *What's that shiny thing in his hand? A knife! I'm getting out of here!* Instead he shrank back in his corner.

Scarface! thought Alvin. *I wish that drum would stop beating, so I could think things through!* He shrank back in his corner.

"I'm over here, mon!" Pim's voice rang through the Swap Shop, clear as a bell. "I'm over here. Come and get me!"

"That's exactly what I'll do, kid." The words were loaded with bitterness. "You've led me all the way here from Eleuthera, but this is the end of the trail. You'll either give it to me now, or *you'll get what old man Pogue got!*"

Scarface advanced cautiously across the darkened room. Not once did he take his eyes off Pim's dusky face. He moved slowly, first one foot then the other, feeling his way along the cleared path that Pim had followed a moment earlier.

When Scarface reached the treadmill he, too, stumbled across the front edge, then caught his balance by flinging out his hands and grabbing the two rails. There was the clatter of metal across the floor.

Scarface climbed up to the center of the treadmill and stood there for a moment looking down at Pim, no more than four feet away.

"I don't need the knife anyway," he whispered venomously. "Not for a small fry like you. I can handle you with my bare hands. Just wait till —"

"NOW!!!!" shouted Alvin from the far corner.

Instantly Shoie flipped the switch and the Swap Shop was bathed in brilliant light from Mr. Ginzburg's spotlights. One was fastened to the wall high in each corner of the room, and all were focused on Scarface.

In the crossfire of blinding light the man instinctively raised his hands to cover his eyes.

Alvin was half-blinded too, but the dark glasses helped considerably. The instant he saw Scarface raise his hands, he flipped the treadmill control switch to speed number four.

Even Alvin was amazed at what happened. One moment the man had been threatening Pim's life; now, temporarily blinded, he staggered backward as the treadmill rolled into life, then flung out his hands to keep his balance. Instinctively he grabbed the rails. By pumping his legs at a fast jog he was just able to keep his feet.

Alvin turned the control switch to speed number five.

The treadmill moved faster. Now Scarface was running along at a brisk pace, glaring blindly down toward Pim, trying desperately to reach the end of the treadmill — and the boy.

"Now, Shoie!" shouted Alvin.

Shoie reached directly above his head, and found the end of the rope that was hanging there. The rope ran up through a pulley Alvin had fastened to the ceiling. From there it ran down to the handle of an old bucket.

Shoie jerked the rope, then jerked it again. And again. And again. The bucket flopped this way and that. Tubby's used engine oil, black as midnight, sloshed out and plummeted down on top of Scarface's head. He glanced up to see the source of the danger. Shoie gave a final jerk. This time the bucket flopped completely upside down. A final gallon of black oil spilled directly down onto the man's upturned face, ran down his neck, and covered his clothing.

"AAAAARRRRGGGGHH! PPTTTTU-UUUIII!" Scarface tried to spit the stuff out of his mouth. At the same time he reached up one hand to wipe his blinded eyes. It was almost a fatal error, for he lost his balance. As he fell forward, he grabbed the rail again. Now his knuckles showed white as he pumped away with his legs.

Alvin turned the control switch up to speed number six.

Scarface gasped as his feet pumped even faster.

"Okay, Shoie!" shouted Alvin.

Shoie grabbed an extension cord from the floor, found the switch, and pulled the chain.

Mrs. Nardulli's big window fan, bolted to a table nearby, hummed into life, then picked up speed. And as it picked up speed, it picked up something else — Jennie Oostermeyer's chicken feathers. The kids had poured the feathers loosely into a big, shallow box behind the powerful fan. And as the fan reached top speed, it began sucking feathers out of the box. They whipped through the blades and shot out of the fan in a huge ball followed by a broad feathery stream.

"OOORRRRRFFF!" Scarface caught a glimpse of the ball of feathers hurtling in his direction and tried to tuck his face behind his right shoulder. The white ball hit him head on. And everywhere the feathers hit, they stuck to the engine oil.

Alvin turned the control switch to speed number seven.

"Okay, Pest!" he hollered.

Daphne was standing on a chair in her corner. Perched on a shelf above her head was Lisa Linkletter's stuffed owl, its dusty wings spread wide. A cord, knotted around the owl's neck ran to a nail in the ceiling above the treadmill.

"WWWHHHOOOOOOOOOOOOO!!!!" hollered Daphne. She gave the owl a tremendous shove off the shelf. It swooped down in an arc toward the floor, then swung upward like a gigantic winged pendulum. And in its talons the owl clutched a paper bag.

At the last moment Scarface saw the owl winging relentlessly toward his head. He could only watch helplessly, his legs pumping for all they were worth, as the owl made its swoop. At the last instant the stuffed bird whizzed past his face, but the paper bag that dangled from the talons struck him smack in the nose.

It was an explosion. The paper bag ripped open, and five pounds of Bernard Bezy's Cut-Rate Itching Powder puffed out into a white ball that enveloped Scarface. When the haze cleared somewhat, Alvin could see the man covered with black oil, white feathers, and powder, dancing like mad.

Alvin turned the control switch to speed number eight.

"Okay, Shoie!" he shouted.

Shoie hurriedly clambered over the hoses and rakes, the boxes of books and plastic flowers, until he was close to the lower edge of the treadmill. The creeper was at his feet. He shoved it into position.

Alvin turned the control switch all the way up to speed number ten.

"Okay, Daphne!" he shouted.

She had the pull-chain in her hand, and instantly gave it a jerk.

It was a good thing the kids were wearing earmuffs. Even then, they were almost deafened by the sound of "The Star-Spangled Banner" coming out of Alvin's tape recorder, playing through the skating rink's old amplifier, and coming out the two gigantic speakers aimed right at Scarface.

Daphne clutched her hands over her earmuffs and danced in pain. Shoie clapped his over his ears and reared back in amazement; he had no idea how Alvin could get so much noise out of such a little tape recorder.

And Alvin, also holding his earmuffs to his ears, watched his enemy as closely as a doctor watches a patient.

The man endured the torture for five, then ten seconds, his face a white and feathery mask. Finally he could stand it no longer. He gave up. He jerked his hands from the rails and clapped them over his ears. At the same time he dropped face down onto the treadmill.

Scarface was, in effect, shot out of a cannon.

The treadmill flung him backwards toward the door of the Swap Shop. Slippery with oil, he slid off the platform and onto the creeper that Shoie had placed there. And the creeper, its wheels well oiled by the kids that afternoon, shot across the floor toward the front door.

It was only a slight miscalculation. The creeper would have missed the doorway by inches and slammed into the wall, but at the last moment Shoie stuck out his foot and gave it a slight shove to the side.

Scarface shot through the doorway, across the drive, and along the sidewalk. The front wheels hit a bump and the creeper sailed up and out across the curb.

Alvin, now in the doorway, gasped at the sight.

Barney Pflug, who sometimes drank too much beer, was just coming around the corner of Maple Street in his pickup truck. Barney saw a feathery white ghost on a bobsled sail across his radiator. He gave up beer for three months.

Scarface, who had a death clutch on the creeper, sailed on. He made his landing all the way across the street. When the creeper struck the curb it stopped instantly. Scarface slid right on across the parkway to the sidewalk. He came to rest at the feet of old Mrs. Beasley, who was walking her dog. The Saint Bernard took one look at Scarface, broke his leash, and ran howling up Maple Street. Mrs. Beasley screamed and screamed.

"Remarkable!" Alvin said silently to his Magnificent Brain. "You've done it again!"

He turned and signaled the Pest to switch off the tape recorder. When he removed his earmuffs he heard the whine of the siren.

The Treasure Is Found!

Daphne couldn't help feeling just a little bit sorry for Scarface. She went inside the Swap Shop and returned with a piece of canvas to cover him. When Scarface saw her approaching he shouted at the police, "Don't let those kids near me! Keep them away! I'll tell you anything, just keep them away!"

And talk he did — eventually.

Dad had been the first to leap from the squad car. He couldn't believe his eyes when he saw the strange feathery figure staggering about, shouting for help and scratching desperately all over his body. When he saw the four kids watching from the front of the Swap Shop, he demanded an explanation.

"Who is this man?" Dad asked sternly, nodding his head toward Scarface. "And who's this boy? Do they belong together? What's been going on inside that shop of yours, Alvin?"

By now a crowd had gathered, first attracted by the booming music that had come from the tape recorder. More arrived every minute, drawn by the squad car's flashing red light.

Mr. Moser, ace reporter for the *Daily Bugle*, came trotting across the street. When he saw Alvin he winked. He had written so many newspaper articles about Alvin's escapades of the past that he knew he was likely to get a big story now. He arrived just in time to hear Alvin's answer to his Dad's question.

"This," said Alvin proudly, taking Pim by the arm, "is a friend of mine — a very close friend named Pim Bethel." He saw the Pest waving belligerently. "And a friend of Daphne and Shoie too. And this" — he nodded his head toward Scarface — "is a man who has been trying to catch Pim. He's also a murderer."

Daphne piped up, "And he's a smuggler and he escaped from the Dade County Jail in Florida, and his name is David Wasco and he uses the aliases Douglas Watley and Gary Warren, and he probably was mean to Pim's mother."

"Whoa," said Dad. "Easy now. Suppose you tell me the whole story, as quickly as you can, Alvin."

Alvin did. He shortened the story wherever possible, but he told the background just as Pim had told it to him. When he described how Scarface had murdered the older man, Dad quietly interrupted just long enough to search Scarface and slip handcuffs on him. He told him he was under arrest on suspicion of murder, and recited his rights to him. Then Dad nodded to Alvin.

When everything was told, Dad said sternly, "You kids should have come to the police immediately."

"Don't blame the others, sir," Pim interjected quietly. "I'm to blame. But I was sure he'd harm my mother if we went to the police."

Mr. Moser was taking notes like mad. Obviously it was the kind of story he liked — a tale of murder on a tropical island, the flight of a boy, and the final entrapment of a criminal by four kids.

"We used a lot of the stuff from the Swap Shop," said Alvin. "We wanted to teach him a lesson — make him look foolish and scare him, so he would never threaten Pim again."

"I think you did just that," Dad said. He had a stern look on his face, but Alvin thought there was a hint of pride in Dad's eyes too. Dad took Scarface, still scratching desperately, by the shoulder and turned him toward the squad car. "Come along. We'll clean you up in the jail."

"Just a minute, Dad." Alvin's voice had taken on a commanding ring. Dad turned, and so did Scarface. "I want to show you something, and I especially want Scarface to see it too. It will prevent him from ever trying to lay his hands on the treasure again."

Alvin paused.

Shoie said, "You know where the treasure is, old bean." It was not a question, but a statement of fact.

"I'm certain I do. First, though, consider this: None of us knew *what* the treasure was all this time, not even Pim. He didn't think he was carrying the treasure, but he was. *He carried it all the way from the Bahamas, without even knowing it.*"

"How could I do that?" Pim asked in surprise.

"How could he do that?" echoed the Pest.

"Come inside the Swap Shop, and I'll explain."

Alvin led the way followed by the other kids, Scarface, the police, and scores of onlookers. Now that the danger was over, Alvin was in complete control of the situation. He leaned one elbow on a rail of the treadmill and resumed his explanation.

"I began thinking about this whole thing a couple of days ago," said Alvin. "Whatever the treasure was, it had to be very, very small, and light in weight. This ruled out coins, or bars of gold or silver. I thought briefly that it might be a diamond, or an emerald. But no — it had to be something the two men found in that sunken ship. And all they'd brought up was a chest with a few old coins and a love letter.

"The more I thought about it, the more I wondered about that letter. It seemed a simple enough message from a girl in England to her sailor boyfriend. First I thought that the letter might not really be a love letter after all — that it might be some very important letter written in code. Even so, it was a letter, and Pim couldn't have carried anything as large as a letter all this way without being aware of it. No, it had to be something else."

Alvin had once visited the courtroom when a criminal trial was under way. Now his voice took on a deeper tone as he imitated the lawyer who had impressed him so much.

"Pim, I now ask you to recall that day on Eleuthera, in your own home. Old Mr. Pogue was on your bed, dying of his stab wounds. Now at that moment where was your lucky shell?"

Pim opened his mouth, then closed it again. He gazed up at the stuffed owl, now dangling by its neck from the ceiling. Finally he said, "On that day, for the first time since my father gave me the shell, I forgot to put it in my pocket." He thought a moment. "And since it wasn't in my pocket, it was on the table beside the bed."

"Were you ever out of the old man's sight?"

"No." A pause. Then, "Yes. I was. I went to the pump for water to clean the blood off Mr. Pogue."

"Then I submit that *the hiding place for the treasure is Pim's lucky shell*. It was available to the dying old man, right beside him on the table. And when he said to Pim, 'Now you have it, and it's yours,' he didn't mean that he had actually handed it over to Pim, but that he'd left it where Pim would find it."

There was absolute silence in the Swap Shop. Every eye was on Pim. Slowly he reached in his pocket and pulled out the shell. He looked down at it. "There is nothing here," he said.

"I wouldn't be so sure," said Alvin. "I also know what the treasure is — and it's there. I found a clue to it here inside the Swap Shop." He walked over to the stack of old books he had acquired from Myron Butz. He flipped through half a dozen until he found the one he wanted.

"This book is titled *A Collector's Guide to Early Stamps of the World*. Let me read a few sentences to you." Alvin was in no hurry. He knew he had everyone's attention as he searched through the pages. Finally he found the passage he wanted.

Triumphantly he read, " 'The earliest postage stamps came into use in Great Britain in 1840. In that year, through the efforts of Sir Rowland Hill, Great Britain issued a one-penny black and a two-penny blue stamp bearing the likeness of Queen Victoria.'"

He put the book back in the carton. "Pim mentioned that Mr. Pogue, among other books on his boat, had a volume on stamp collecting. He probably looked up this love-letter stamp in the book, and found that it was worth a fortune." He looked across at Pim. "Pim, may I borrow your lucky shell for a moment?"

Pim reached out his hand. When he placed the shell in Alvin's palm, their fingers touched for a moment. The two boys looked into each other's eyes. At the same moment they both smiled — a secret smile that only the other could see.

Alvin held up the shell. He looked across at Scarface. "I want you to watch everything, so you'll have no reason any longer ever to bother Pim or his mother again."

Alvin picked up a small piece of wire off the floor and fashioned it into a hook.

He slipped the hook far back into the recesses of the shell. Then he pulled it slowly out.

There was something attached to the hook — a torn piece of paper peeking from the

151

shell. Very carefully Alvin took it between his thumb and fingernail, and pulled it all the way out. For a moment he looked at it, then held it up for everyone to see.

"You'll notice," he said, "that the stamp bears the likeness of a woman with a crown on her head. The stamp also is blue. It probably is the first stamp of Queen Victoria — in fact, the first stamp ever issued. As such, it perhaps is priceless, but in any case is worth many thousands of dollars. That is the treasure everyone has been after — a postage stamp that is worth much more than a pirate's treasure in gold and silver."

Alvin fixed his gaze on Scarface. "I want you" — he jabbed his finger at the man — "to pay particular attention to what happens here. I'm now giving this stamp into the care of the police. Pim will no longer be carrying it — ever. Under no circumstances — even after you leave prison, or even if you should again escape — can you ever get your hands on it by threatening Pim's mother. And if you should ever appear here in the future, we'll have even more fun with you than we did this time."

Scarface looked up at the owl swinging above his head. He looked down at the feathers that covered his body. He began scratching with both hands.

Alvin dropped the stamp into his father's hand.

Dad cleared his throat. "Pim, the first thing we must do is contact your mother, so you'll know she's all right, and she'll know you are safe. Meanwhile, I'll put this valuable little scrap of paper" — he held up the postage stamp — "into the police vault, where it will be safe until the court decides how to dispose of it." He smiled at Pim. "But I think I can predict the court's decision. The old man was rightful owner until he died. He gave it to you. Therefore, you are now the owner, and when it is sold, you will receive the money."

Every eye in the Swap Shop was on Pim. For a moment he stood motionless. Then his eyes moved, first to Alvin, then to Daphne, then to Shoie. He smiled, a grave little smile. He looked around the Swap Shop, slowly, carefully, as though to memorize each thing in its place. Finally his glance came to rest on the box of old books. When Pim spoke, it was so softly that it was difficult to hear his words.

"That little stamp may be worth lots of

money, as you say it is. If so, and the money is mine, I know what I'll do with it. I'll call all the kids of Eleuthera together. I'll tell them that we will build a library. And that tiny scrap of paper will pay for all the construction materials. But we will build it *together*, so each of us is a part of it. Then, when the building is finished and the shelves are up, I'll use the rest of the money to buy books — hundreds of books, perhaps thousands of books, to fill those shelves."

Daphne's eyes were still shining. There was a fresh tear in each. She brushed them aside. "Oh, Pim."

Pim had gone to the police station, as Dad said, "for a few minutes to straighten everything out." Then Dad was bringing him home to stay overnight. The next day they would arrange his transportation back to Eleuthera.

Alvin, the Pest, and Shoie, were still in the Swap Shop. Alvin looked around at the oil-stained floor, at the layer of feathers that covered everything, at all the junk scattered about.

"We'll clean it up tomorrow," he said quietly. He didn't sound very enthusiastic.

A high little voice popped up from just inside the doorway. "Hey, Alvin. Lookey here!"

It was Turkey Otto, and in his hand he held Alvin's old glass toothbrush container.

Alvin walked over. He looked inside the glass.

"It's Elmira, Alvin. She's a great little ant. And I've taught her a new trick. Look! She can stand on her head!" He held the glass upright. Elmira fell to the bottom. She remained there, resting on her feelers, looking for all the world as though she were standing on her head. Turkey gobbled.

Alvin stroked the glass. "Elmira, you're something else," he said. He gazed round the Swap Shop, at the tremendous number of items — a good deal of junk, he realized, but also many items of value — that they had acquired without paying a penny. That they had acquired with one trained ant. "You're something else, Elmira," he repeated softly. He looked at the Pest and Shoie.

"What would you think," he said, "if we had a public auction next Saturday? What if we sold all this stuff? And then what if we used any money we make to buy more books for Pim's library?"

"More books for Pim's library," repeated Daphne, her eyes still shining.

"Great idea, old bean," said Shoie.

Alvin reached out and stroked the glass once more. "Thanks, Elmira," he said in a whisper.

The little black ant stood on her head and waved her hind legs.